CASES

OF

KARMA

by

Brandy Lynette

BK
ROYSTON
Publishing

BK Royston Publishing
Jeffersonville, IN   47131
http://www.bkroystonpublishing.com
bkroystonpublishing@gmail.com

ISBN: 978-1-967282-79-1

English Standard Version (ESV) - The ESV® Bible (The
Holy Bible, English Standard Version®), © 2001 by
Crossway, a publishing ministry of Good News
Publishers. ESV Text Edition: 2025.

King James Version (KJV) - Public Domain

New International Version NIV - Holy Bible, New
International Version®, NIV® Copyright ©1973, 1978,
1984, 2011 by Biblica, Inc.® Used by permission. All
rights reserved worldwide.

New Living Translation (NLT) - Holy Bible, New Living
Translation, copyright © 1996, 2004, 2015 by Tyndale
House Foundation. Used by permission of Tyndale House
Publishers, Inc., Carol Stream, Illinois 60188. All
rights reserved.

Printed in the United States of America

Dedication

To anyone who's carried shame for far too long—

This story is yours.

May you release what tried to bury you, leave the past where it belongs, and remember:

You are not your past.

You are the story guilt never saw coming.

Acknowledgements

To God, my Redeemer, my refuge, my reminder. Every word in this book was shaped by a grace I didn't earn but received anyway. Thank You for never letting go, even when I was ready to.

To Gabriel, aka Tre', Brayden, and Christian—your love grounds me. You are my reasons to rise, to fight, and to remember that God's grace is truly sufficient. You are the best chapters of my life.

To my family—thank you for your prayers, patience, and presence during this journey. Especially to my mom, dad, and grandparents, whose lives and legacies still echo through mine. This story is rooted in what I witnessed, what I survived, and what I chose to rise above.

To my village—my sisters and friends who doubled as therapists, accountability partners, and cheerleaders: thank you for letting me cry, dream, process, and create out loud. I love y'all deeply.

To my readers—thank you for opening these pages and finding pieces of yourself between the lines. May this story remind you: brokenness doesn't disqualify you. It creates the perfect opportunity for God to rebuild, restore, and reveal a marvelous new version of you.

And finally, to the version of me who almost quit—

Look what wonders God did with the wreckage.

Table of Contents

Why I Wrote This

I didn't write this book because I had all the answers.
I wrote it because I was brave enough to ask questions.

Questions like:
What if shame could speak?
What if trauma doesn't just live in our memories, but in our choices?
What if grace is the only thing strong enough to rewrite the story of a broken heart?

Cases of Karma was born out of my own reckoning. With faith, with pain, with the patterns that repeated themselves in silence until I finally named them out loud. I've known what it's like to feel haunted by your past. To carry guilt that doesn't just weigh on you, but rewrites how you love, how you parent, and how you see yourself in the mirror.

This story is not a confession.
It's a declaration.

A declaration that trauma may shape you, but it doesn't define you. That brokenness isn't the end. If you allow it, it can be the beginning of a breakthrough. You can fall. You can

fail. You can lose yourself completely…
and yet still be worthy of redemption.

I wrote this for the one who's been
surviving on autopilot.
For the one who looks strong on the
outside but is unraveling on the
inside.
For anyone who's ever whispered, *"Am I
too far gone?"*

You're not.

You are the story still being written.
And if you let it, grace will provide a
strong finish for you.

Welcome to **Cases of Karma.**
Let's begin again—together.

Prologue

Tiffeny

For a minute, it was all a blur. I heard distant chatter but couldn't identify to whom the voices belonged. Everything was so… fuzzy. I saw images of people standing in the doorway, but I couldn't make out who they were. Tossing and turning, I fought to open my eyes. Something was connected…

"Wait."

I felt around the bed where I lay, still unable to bring my vision into focus. "What is this? Wires? Cords? What the… tubes?"

I was covered by a heavy cloth and surrounded by what felt like metal or thick plastic bars. Had I been kidnapped?

Trying to remain calm, I could feel my heart begin to race. Moving my hands over my mouth, I realized I was wearing what felt like an oxygen mask. All of my movements felt slow and strained. I was overwhelmed with emotion and questions. I could hear machines beeping around me; it was all so overstimulating. I was beginning to feel frustrated and couldn't help but feel panicked. It seemed as though everything around me was a blurred, indistinguishable haze, while a profound drowsiness weighed me down. It made every thought and every movement an immense effort.

"What in the world is going on? Have I been drugged? Where am I?"

The more anxious and fearful I became from not having control over my body and mind, the faster the machines beeped. I fought hard to break free from what felt like a comatose state. My heart was pounding so hard that I thought my chest might explode. Tears filled my eyes. And my son? Wait; where is my son? I've got to get up and get to my child! Before I suffered a complete mental collapse, I tried to pull it together.

"Calm down, Tiffeny. Just breathe, girl. You're alive. That's a plus. I think."

I wiggled my toes and moved my head left to right, just to make sure I wasn't paralyzed.

"Seriously! What's going on?"

As I continued my attempts to decompress, I was reminded of the breathing exercises I'd learned in therapy. I decided to focus completely on my breathing, dismissing the fear of not remembering where I was, and just… breathe—long, steady, calm breaths. I paused and inhaled slowly, counting, one… two… three… hold. That's it, gentle now. I inhaled, counted, held, and released, repeating the cycle. And then, like magic, it worked. The machines slowed. My heart rate eased. My eyes opened. My vision, though still blurry, began to focus. The room was dimly lit, but I could see it was empty. The two people I'd heard in the doorway were no longer there.

Not long after… I remembered.

"Arghhh," I groaned.

Frustration washed over me as my past and present came crashing together. I continued my deep breathing exercises, and finally, I remembered the chain of events that led to me lying here in this bed.

Taking one last deep breath in, I exhaled, and the tears came, not because of the pain, but because I remembered.

I remembered everything.

The left side of my stomach throbbed with intense pain, shooting through my entire left side and wrapping around to my back. I ran my hand over the now bandaged area and flinched. It was tender to the touch. In an attempt to get a glimpse of the wound, I moved my hand slowly toward the area. Even stretching my neck downward brought excruciating pain. Falling back in instant regret, my mind wandered.

Is this what I get for trying? I really thought this time would be different. Who was I kidding? What made me think I deserved anything better?

"Ha," I let out a glib, humorless chuckle.

There wasn't a thing funny about my current situation. Here I was, lying in a hospital bed, connected to machines that monitored my vitals, ensuring I was alive.

And all I could hear was my grandma's voice, "Baby, you've got to be careful about what roots you lay down in this

world." She always quoted Galatians
6:7: "Do not be deceived; God cannot
be mocked. A man reaps what he sows."
So let's just say I wasn't surprised.

You know the saying, "Karma's a…"

Chapter 1

Tiffeny

Proverbs 11:14-15(NLT), "Without wise leadership, a nation falls; there is safety in having many advisers."

I sat on the wide, two-seater hunter green loveseat with thick cushions, while she sat in a luxurious, deep, feather-gray high-backed chair directly across from me.

The office always smelled like a blend of soft lavender and vanilla, with a hint of mint leaves. I loved the whole setup she had going on in here. There were throw pillows, blinged-out mirrors, lavish light fixtures, and a large area rug that I hated stepping on every time I walked in, because it was just that gorgeous. Her office, or maybe I should say suite, was fancy. Like, *fancy* fancy. Sophisticated, modern, chic, and still professional all at once.

Her desk was all glass, supported by sleek black metal stands. It had this faint blue tint and sparkled even without sunlight. I swear, the thing looked like it came straight out of some boutique furniture store in Italy or Paris. Custom-designed, like it was made to fit her body exactly. No way

I'd fit comfortably behind that thing.
All of *these* hips? Please.

Now don't get me wrong, I'm not fat.
But compared to me, Dr. Johnson—Hope
Daysianique Johnson, sis was skinny.
She wasn't bad looking, but she
could've stood to pick up a few extra
pieces of fried chicken with cornbread,
potato salad, maybe a little bit of
sweet potatoes, and a side of peach
cobbler if you asked me. And then lie
down right after. It's important to go
lie down. Some people don't realize
that's how you get the weight to stick
to your bones.

Dr. Johnson looked like one of those
health nuts who runs after every meal.
Sis couldn't have been over a size 2.
But her energy? Always calm, always
poised. Still, she had this light about
her. Like, when our sessions were over,
I always felt just a little more ready
to live life one more day. That's why I
kept coming back. Mondays and Thursdays
at 6 p.m. like clockwork.

In the beginning, I had my doubts.
Coming to some stranger, putting all my
business out there? Nah. You couldn't
have paid me to do this back in the
day. But when Pastor David and First
Lady Elaine Blackwell recommended her,
I figured it couldn't hurt.

Now? I can't get enough of it. I always feel lighter afterward, like I've released something I didn't even know I was holding. Healing isn't a switch you just flip. It's a process, especially when you start digging up stuff you've spent years burying. It hurts. But that's how you know it's working.

"Do you consider yourself a selfish person?" she asked.

I told her that people love to slap labels on me just because I tend to choose myself. My momma raised me to know that this world is a dog-eat-dog world. If I didn't prioritize me, who would? *PERIOD.*

"If people want to call that selfish, then so be it," I replied. "I can't control what they think. They're gonna talk regardless. That's exactly why I've decided to always choose me."

I knew she caught the irritation in my voice. This subject? Always a sensitive one. I didn't choose this life—it chose me. After the pain, the rejection, the disappointment and what I've witnessed... I made a vow. Never again, would I let someone leave me that vulnerable.

"I'm not saying it's wrong or selfish to feel that way," she said gently.

"I'm simply asking *if you* consider
yourself a selfish person."

"Well… I guess." I shrugged.

"Is this because of the relationship
you had with the married man?"

I let out a long sigh.

I didn't want to talk about him.
Josiah. The name alone made me feel sad
and mad at the same time. I'll admit, I
don't always make the best decisions.
But I'm not a bad person. I have a
heart. I care. And Josiah… he was one
of those people.

I shut my eyes, hoping she'd take the
hint. She did.

We had about fifteen minutes left in
the session, and I figured she wouldn't
press the issue. She took a slow breath
and asked, "Okay, what are your goals
for this week? Do you want to start
identifying areas where you feel you
haven't made the best decisions, and
then next session, we can explore how
to begin letting some of that go?"

I rolled my eyes. I was over it.

"Sure. I guess."

"Wonderful!" she chirped. Her voice flipped right back to that upbeat tone she used whenever she felt like we made a breakthrough.

Truth was I was annoyed. But I still took her assignments seriously, no matter how much they bothered me. I had to be real with myself; they worked.

Even off the top of my head, I could think of a few choices I wasn't proud of. But not one of them, not a single one, included my son.

The way he came into this world might not have been the most ideal, but I would never, not for one second, regret having Joshua.

That boy right there makes my heart smile.

If I'm being completely honest, it wasn't until he arrived that I started looking at my life differently. I realized, almost instantly, that I wanted to do better.

Not for people.

Not even for me.

But for Joshua Tore' Williams.

Chapter 2

Cameron

Proverbs 6:27(NLT) says, *"Can a man scoop a flame into his lap and not have his clothes catch on fire?"* Or, like my momma used to say, "Boy, you keep playing with fire, you're gonna get burned."

"Stop playing these games with me, Regina! That's not fair, and you know it!" I snapped, yanking the phone from my ear and stuffing it deep into my pocket.

I looked up, staring out of the 36 X 48 aluminum picture window, letting my eyes settle on the golden streaks of the sunset. For a moment, I let go of the chaos and just breathed in the beauty of God's creation. But it didn't last long. I realized she'd hung up on me again. Regina was getting on my last nerve.

This back-and-forth nonsense, using our son as a pawn, was draining any ounce of respect I had left for her. She needed to grow up. Only immature, petty girls pull stunts like that, using their own child to control a situation.

But she was about to learn I don't play when it comes to my son.

I may not have made the best choices in life, but on everything I love, I love my son Carson with every fiber of my being. From the depths of my soul, that boy is my heart. Regina? She's just bitter because we didn't work out. And I'm not saying that to make myself look good or play the victim. I'm saying it because it's the truth. Flat out.

Regina and I were a thing for maybe a month, over nine years ago. I met her at my homeboy's wedding. She was one of the bridesmaids, I was a groomsman. We didn't walk together, but that didn't stop her from shooting her shot. Right there at the rehearsal, she stepped in while I was chatting with the bridesmaid I was paired with.

"Excuse me! Rude!" the other girl snapped. "We were talking."

Regina ignored her completely, looked me dead in my face, and told me my brown skin was smooth like butter and that she loved my million-dollar smile.

I won't lie, the girl I was talking to was cute, with a pretty face, thick in the hips, booty for days. But Regina? Regina was more my type. Slim-thick, long hair with blonde highlights, flawless light-brown skin, perfect smile, and a confidence that didn't flinch. Yeah, anyone who knew me knew I had a thing for redbones. And Regina's sexiness, combined with her assertiveness? Shorty had me intrigued.

Her whole energy said, *I'm what you want*. And in that moment? She was right. She knew she was bad and didn't care who was watching. Just like that, I was hooked.

Thing is, deep down, I knew she was probably trouble.

Anybody that bold, with that much unapologetic energy pulsing through her, had to be toxic. The kind of woman who doesn't just enter a room but commands it, because she knows she's a ten.

And me? I walked straight into the storm like it was sunlight.

We hooked up, had sex a few times, and like I tend to do, I started drifting. What can I say? I lose interest quickly. That's on me.

She let me hit the same night we met, after the wedding reception. And yeah, I know that says a lot about both of us. I'm not claiming to be perfect. I've made some dumb choices. But after Carson was born, everything changed. Life became more than sex, parties, and clout.

I'm not bragging, but I was what you'd call a catch. I had a thriving career as VP at a Black-owned marketing firm in Chicago. Double Master's in Marketing and Business, a minor in HR, and a DEI certificate. I loved my job. We worked with R&B and hip-hop artists, major Black-owned franchises, hosted some of the hottest events in the city, traveled the country—basically living the good life.

But Regina? She thought having my baby would trap me. She played herself.

Because if there's one thing about me, ain't nobody making me do nothing that I don't want to do, and that's on everything I love.

We used protection the first few times, then decided to share STD test results. Everything came back clean. We went raw. That was her idea. Regina said she was on birth control, had her alarm set and everything to make sure she took it. She swore she was never late, and it would take a miracle for her to get pregnant—her words, not mine.

A few months later, she told me she might be pregnant. I didn't even believe it. None of it made sense.

I tried to have an honest conversation about abortion, even said I'd cover the cost.

She lost it. Cursed me out seven ways from Sunday and hung up on me.

The truth? I never saw myself as a family man. I've always loved kids, but I wasn't ready. Not then. And definitely not with her.

When it came time for her to have the baby, Regina said she was still mad at me for even mentioning abortion. That's why she blocked me from being at the hospital. She and I both know that was a lie. She wanted to move in with me and be a couple, because she was "the mother of my son."

She called me selfish. A terrible person. Said people looked at her with pity, thinking she was just another single mom who got knocked up by some random dude and ended up on food stamps and Medicaid.

She was embarrassed, ashamed even, that she didn't have a ring on her finger.

I reminded her that's something she should've thought about before deciding to keep the baby.

Still, I heard her. I considered it. But I couldn't marry her just because she was having my child. That wouldn't be fair to her, the baby, or myself. I didn't love Regina like that. I respected her as the mother of my child, but she could never be my wife.

There were too many red flags. Especially when I asked her to wait until after the baby was born. I wanted to see how things went with us. Well, it was obviously the right move on my part. This girl got impatient and threw a whole ugly, immature temper tantrum. She even gave me an ultimatum, threatening to keep me from my son. She said she and Carson were a package deal. That right there sealed it for me. Regina would never be Mrs. Cameron Landry. And that's on everything I love.

When Carson was born, she didn't even tell me she was in labor. I found out after getting tagged in some messy social media post by her friends.

After trying to reach her multiple times, she finally called back and said I could come see "him." I heard that word *him,* and my heart melted. She never found out the gender because she wanted it to be a surprise. I didn't protest. I hadn't even seen him yet, but I felt proud. Another Landry to carry our name.

She turned the camera on him during FaceTime. Man… I knew then he'd be trouble with the ladies. Light peanut butter-brown skin, big hazel eyes, dark curly hair like mine, and full lips like his mama. When I finally held my son in my arms? I was done. Completely and totally in love. Instantly. No hesitation.

But every visit to see Carson came with strings attached. Regina wanted to take family photos, post us on social media like we were some happy couple. One time, she came downstairs in lingerie, trying to seduce me while I was there to see my son. MAN, this chick was crazy.

I had already made things clear. I'm here for Carson. That's it.

But it was never enough for her. I've never missed a child support payment. Anything extra Carson needed? I got it. Regina didn't spend a dime. I tried to set a regular schedule. But Regina? She wanted full control.

And now? Every time she doesn't get her way, she uses my son as leverage.

She was definitely a lesson I had to learn the hard way.

Chapter 3

Tiffeny

"You said you've had several relationships with men who were already involved with someone else—"

"Aht—aht," I cut Dr. Johnson off mid-sentence. "I said *situationships*. Not all were relationships. There's a difference."

"My apologies," she replied, calm as ever. "Several *situationships* with men who were already involved with other women. When was your first encounter, and how did it start?"

My eyes drifted to the ceiling as I let out a slow, heavy sigh. I wasn't in the mood for this. Not today. I didn't feel like digging up old messes and explaining myself to someone, even a therapist who might not get it.

"Look," I started. "I don't want to be judged."

Dr. Johnson leaned forward slightly. "Tiffeny, you know me better than that. This is a no-judgment zone. Your thoughts are your thoughts, and your feelings are your feelings. What I may think or feel about them is irrelevant and nonexistent in this space. I'm just here to help you sort through what *you* feel. So… continue."

I sat there, quiet for about a minute, letting her words settle. Then I took a breath and opened up.

"I know people get offended by the way I go about my 'situationships'. They say it shows a lack of respect for myself and other women." I rolled my eyes. "And I beg to differ. Especially when it comes to *me.*"

I crossed one leg over the other and rested my hands in my lap.

The first time I got involved with a married man, I didn't even know he was still married. I met him at church and he wasn't wearing a wedding ring. After we'd started seeing each other for a while, he later told me he and his wife were taking space. She didn't even go to the same church. So how was I supposed to know?

I paused for a beat, and like clockwork, Dr. Johnson leaned in with a gentle question.

"You said '*still* married'. So… you were aware that he was married at one point?"

"Yes," I admitted. "I guess I didn't ask for clarity because… deep down, I didn't want to know."

The confession hung in the air.

"When he started giving me attention, it was so comforting, so refreshing. I hadn't felt that kind of energy or connection with someone… ever. He was handsome, talented, and intelligent. I don't know a single woman at that church who didn't think that man was fine."

I waited for Dr. Johnson to say something, but she didn't. Just gave me that soft, unreadable stare of hers. It wasn't judgment, just quiet space. And honestly, I needed it.

Because I still didn't understand how I'd ended up being *the villain* in everyone else's story.

They disrespected and devalued their own union first. *They* let their commitment crumble. And yet somehow, I became the cautionary tale of Jezebel. The homewrecker.

How on *God's* green earth was that all on *me*?

I remember walking into church and feeling the stares hot, cold, and sideways. Men mean-mugging. Women whispering. And even their bad little kids glaring at me like they knew my business. I blame the parents talking around or *with* their kids like gossip is family bonding time. Got these little humans thinking they can try me.

Still, at the end of the day, it was my life. Mine, not theirs, not anybody else's. Who I got involved with had nothing to do with the congregation, the choir, or Sister Barbara, who passed out judgment like programs at the Pastor's Appreciation Service.

I never *set out* to steal anyone's man. That was never the mission. But sometimes… it just *happens* like that. I went with the flow. That's all.

And honestly? He's the only man I ever knowingly got involved with who was married; he's the father of my child. The others? Two of them were in long-term relationships. And both of them lied. They never mentioned they had someone. Truthfully? I didn't ask.

People always throw that question at me like a weapon. *Is this how you'd want to be treated? If you were in a relationship, would you want your man stepping out on you?*

Of course, I'd say no. Nobody wants to be disrespected like that. But let's be real…

A part of us feels like it's going to happen anyway. Right?

People cheat. People lie. They choose themselves over loyalty every day. So why should *I* carry the shame? Why should *I* be the one left holding guilt that doesn't entirely belong to me?

Nobody else seems to be paying attention to 1 Corinthians 10:24(NLT), "Don't be concerned for your own good but for the good of others." Look around! Everyone's still walking around with their same selfish ways!

Dr. Johnson finally leaned back, folding her hands in her lap, her voice calm but direct.

"Tiffeny, I hear your frustration. And I understand why you feel misunderstood, why you feel like people have been quicker to point fingers than to ask *why*. But I want you to consider something."

I narrowed my eyes slightly, arms crossed now, bracing myself.

"What if," she continued, "what you've described isn't really about the men…

or even the women they were with. What if it's about *you* and what those situations gave you in the moment?"

I scoffed, "Gave me? Like what?"

"Power. Attention. Emotional validation. Maybe even a sense of belonging."

I blinked slowly, lips tightening.

"You said earlier that it felt comforting when Josiah gave you attention," she went on. "That it had been the only time that you'd felt that kind of energy from someone. That tells me the need was already there. The loneliness… the longing."

I didn't say anything. My jaw clenched a little, but I let her keep going.

"You're not a villain, Tiffeny. But I also don't think you're completely free from responsibility, either. You didn't ask questions. Not because you didn't care, but because you didn't want the answer to interrupt the fantasy."

That one stung.

"And I'm not judging," she added quickly. "I'm asking you to look underneath it all. What were you craving? What were you avoiding? And why did it feel safer to be the 'other woman' than to be someone who was fully chosen?"

My eyes welled up. I wasn't expecting that question. I hated how much it landed.

"Because," I whispered, swallowing hard, "if I were the other woman, the understanding was already there on both sides that there were no expectations of commitment, leaving no chance of me getting hurt."

There it was.

"That makes sense," she said softly. "That's survival. That's self-protection. But is that the life you want to keep building? A life built on staying one foot out the door?"

I looked away.

"I don't know," I muttered. "I just know I've been tired for a long time."

Her silence this time was warm and compassionate.

"You deserve more than being someone's secret, Tiffeny. You deserve to be loved in the open. Fully. Without shame. But to get there, you have to start by loving *yourself* that way."

She let the words settle. No pressure. Just presence.

I exhaled, deep and shaky.

"You think I can change?" I asked, almost too soft to hear.

"I *know* you can," she said. "But the better question is do *you* think you're worth the kind of love that doesn't require you to be somebody's secret?"

I didn't answer. Not yet. But I felt something crack open inside me. Just a little.

Maybe for the first time, I wanted to believe the answer could be yes.

As I sit and reflect on Dr. Johnson's words, I'm reminded of *Philippians 2 verse 3-5 (NLT)*, "Don't be selfish; don't try to impress others. Be humble, thinking of others as better than yourselves. Don't look out only for your own interests, but take an interest in others, too. You must have the same attitude that Christ Jesus had."

That verse hit different that day.

It clung to my spirit like a quiet truth I'd been running from.

Selfish ambition… vain conceit… OR value others… the mindset of Jesus… Is this really possible?

I shifted in my seat, uncomfortable.

Because if I'm honest, I've been looking out for me, protecting myself, guarding my heart, and getting mine before someone else took it. I convinced myself that if I didn't ask the hard questions, like, "Are *you married?* or "Are *you romantically involved with someone?"* or better yet, "*Does someone believe that they are in a romantic relationship with you?"* then I wouldn't have to deal with the answers and I could stay in the fantasy a little while longer.

What would it look like to value myself and others the way God values us? I asked myself.

Not by settling for half-love.

Not by sneaking into shadows and calling it intimacy.

Not by calling something a "situationship" just so I won't have to own that what I was involved in was empty, void of any real value or meaning for my future. Then, I wouldn't have to admit that deep down, I want more.

I closed my eyes and whispered a simple prayer, not a fancy one, just a real one.

"God… help me unlearn what survival taught me. Help me to want more than what I've been settling for. Show me how to love like You… starting with myself."

And for the first time in a long time, I didn't feel ashamed for wanting something real. I just hoped it wasn't too late.

Chapter 4

Cameron

It wasn't until college that I truly got to experience the female species. I never dated in high school. I had crushes, plenty, but none of the girls gave me the time of day. And to be honest, I stayed pretty busy with football, debate team, Black Student Union, and church. I kept my head down and my schedule full.

Most of my friends like to joke that my body finally caught up with my head. Yes, I had a big head back in the day. Everybody wants to be a comedian.

Suddenly, the same girls who used to walk past me were now trying to shoot their shot. It was crazy because it felt like it came out of nowhere. But that shift, that sudden surge of attention, turned me into something I never expected, a dog.

And not just a little one, either. A full-blooded, tail-wagging, street-roaming mutt.

It's nothing but the grace of God that I didn't catch fleas aka an STD. I was always careful about protection, though. Always used a condom. But

still, the way I treated those women?
It wasn't right.

I took everything they gave, knowing
full well most of them were hoping it
would turn into something more. I told
myself I was honest with them from the
jump, that I'd laid it all out in the
beginning. *"I'm not looking for
anything serious."* They always said
they were cool with it. They'd nod and
smile and tell me they understood.

Until we had sex.

That's when everything would change.
Suddenly, they wanted more. More of my
time. More attention. They wanted
dates. Calls. Texts. They wanted me to
care.

And I didn't care. Not really.

I told myself it was their fault for
catching feelings. But deep down, I
knew the truth. I was careless with
hearts that weren't mine to mishandle.

There was one woman that made me
reconsider my behavior, briefly. Senior
year in college, things got dark. Her
name was Kierra.

We had a good time, or so I thought,
until I reminded her again that I
wasn't looking for anything serious. I

had plans. I was focused. I couldn't afford distractions, no matter how fine the woman was. Kierra didn't take it well. Things escalated fast. She started showing up places uninvited, sending crazy text messages and wild voicemails. This girl was making scenes that not only embarrassed me, but should have made her feel mortified. She even threatened to commit suicide if I didn't take her back. It got bad enough that I had to file a formal complaint with the Dean. She ended up being removed from campus.

I later heard she transferred to a nearby college to finish her senior year.

It was ugly. Messy. And honestly, it had me shook.

I hated that I had to get my parents involved, because when I finally explained everything to my mom, she went quiet on the phone. For a long time.

I sat there with that silence eating at me until she finally said, *"Boy… Matthew 7:12, Do to others whatever you would like them to do to you. This is the essence of all that is taught in the law and the prophets."*

Then she got quiet again, and when she finally spoke, her voice was thick with disappointment.

"Cameron Johnathan Landry, I raised you better than this. I told you about playing with people's emotions. That's a dangerous game. You can't just run around hurting people and think the Lord doesn't see. The universe has a way of bringing everything full circle. You reap what you sow, baby. You. Reap. What. You. Sow! Do better."

I could hear the emphasis on that last part and the seriousness in her tone. And all I could say was, *"Yes, ma'am."*

I knew she was right. I knew better, but I justified my actions because I had needs.

After college, I gave a few other relationships a real shot. I really did. That, however, was short-lived. But if I'm being honest, self-diagnosed, of course, I'd somehow turned into a serial monogamist.

I was a one-woman man, at least in theory. I'd stopped juggling multiple women at one time. I didn't cheat. And I definitely didn't mess around with anyone who was taken, married or otherwise. People who stepped out in relationships were despicable to me. Flat out.

Still, I always managed to find something wrong. She was too demanding. Too needy. Too intense. Just too much for me or my circumstances. So, none of them ever lasted longer than six months to a year.

Meanwhile, most of my boys from the college football squad were married. Settled. Kids. Mortgages. Cookouts with couples' game night vibes.

They clown me all the time about how I just can't seem to settle down.

And truthfully? Since I'm unable to pinpoint what my issue is, in theory, it's not me, it's them.

Maybe I've been chasing an illusion, comparing every situation to something that might not even exist.

My boy, Tarique, suggested I look at my family to try to identify what my commitment issues might be. But my parents' relationship… it was solid. Loving. Built on mutual respect, sacrifice, faith, *real* faith, not just Sunday morning faith. My father still looked at my mom like she was the best decision he ever made. My mom, she honored him in return, not like in some outdated gender role type of way, but she honored him because he led with love. I always felt like, in turn, that honor, love, and respect was reciprocated.

They weren't perfect. But they had a rhythm, a sacred bond that made everything feel possible. And maybe I put that on a pedestal. Maybe I measured every woman I dated against that standard, looking for something I wasn't even mature enough to sustain myself.

Maybe… that's part of the problem. Who knows?

Chapter 5

Tiffeny

Although I had a breakthrough session
with Dr. Johnson last week, the simple
thought of believing I deserved
something more or better still felt
thousands of miles away, completely
unattainable.

Yet, I could still hear Lady Blackwell
from my church back home encouraging me
with Isaiah 43:18-19(NIV), *"Forget the
former things; do not dwell on the
past. See, I am doing a new thing! Now
it springs up; do you not perceive it?
I am making a way in the wilderness and
streams in the wasteland."*

Lady Blackwell knew I struggled with
things from my past and would often
remind me that I was worthy of love
even after she learned of the mistakes
I'd made. Still, I stood patiently,
waiting on the other shoe to drop.

I had just left work and was headed to
meet one of my co-workers at a local
marketing event downtown. It was a
Black-owned venue that stayed popping
on weekends, playing hip hop and R&B.
They also featured local artists, with
paintings on display, and some nights
they'd host open mic performances.

As crazy as some might think Chicago is, I loved this place. I haven't lived here long. I relocated from California about a year ago. The fiasco between me and my baby daddy caused such a ripple in my relationships with everyone at church and the city that I just felt it would be easier to start over somewhere fresh.

Joshua, he's six now. He still visits his dad as often as he can. Our plan is to keep it consistent every summer and spring break. His dad has been touring more lately, preaching and singing, so whenever he's out here or near the area, I non-grudgingly take Joshua to see him.

My co-worker, Leanna, wanted me to take the stage tonight during open mic. She had noticed I'd been stressed and on edge the past few weeks and felt if I let my frustrations out in song, I'd release some of that pent-up energy. I'm not going to lie, it truly helped.

I'd only visited this place once before when we first moved here. I loved every bit of it—the energy, the vibe, the eclecticism of the people. It was dope. The vocalists were incredible, and the spoken word artists were spitting fire. I couldn't wait to share.

I've never been shy, even back home in Cali. I used to lead worship at church regularly, which is actually how Josiah and I got close.

Tonight, I sang an original piece, titled *Echoes of My Own Undoing*. This song came from a place of understanding the many mistakes I was making in life and how I recognized the self-sabotage I was willingly putting myself through. It was to the point that I truly believed I'd messed up too deeply to be forgiven.

The lyrics went something like this:

Your face, your smile, your scent, I dared

To love every single part of you, a forbidden affair. They say I'd rather be wrong if loving you ain't right, but tonight, every touch, every kiss, your very essence blows my mind.

Where will this leave me, when I've already come undone?

But I can't run, your magnetic energy has me,

Knowing full well it's limerence and false love.

Whenever I sing, I get lost in time, especially if I'm singing gospel. I imagine it's just me and Christ. Lying at His feet, I would pour my soul out to Him.

Tonight, I closed my eyes and completely lost myself in the lyrics… and in the memory that surfaced, the one I usually keep shoved in the very back of my mind.

I was sixteen again.

Standing in the hallway of our apartment, eavesdropping on my mom and her boyfriend. He was yelling again. He'd been caught cheating… again. Just like all the others before him. Just like all the other failed relationships, she tolerated it again.

Mom had many relationships after my dad left her for another man. I couldn't understand why she felt like any of this was acceptable. She believed she had to accept anything, regardless of how it was delivered.

He screamed and cursed at her like she was worthless. When he was triggered, he became dangerous. I watched as he poured a can of beer over her head, letting it spill onto the floor, then demanded she clean up the mess. After

that, he hurled names at her, words I
didn't even understand back then.

My mom just stood there, arms folded,
biting the inside of her cheek like she
was trying to disappear inside herself.

I remember watching from the shadows as
she nodded, pretending not to care.
Finally, he stormed out and slammed the
door so hard, the walls shook. He'd be
back. This one always seemed to come
back. After a few days of doing
whatever, he did. When he needed a
"break", he'd return, and Momma always
welcomed him back with open arms.

Then she did the thing that broke me
every time.

She turned around, wiped her face
quickly, and smiled when she saw me.
"It's okay, baby," she said, like
nothing had happened. "Go do your
homework."

I never told her I heard everything.
Never asked her why she stayed. But
part of me learned right then,
sometimes, you have to take what love
gives you, even if it hurts. And often
times, you have to just ignore the
hurt. Otherwise, you're left with
nothing.

After I finished the song, I opened my eyes and a single tear fell down my face. I looked around the room, and without realizing it, I had everyone's attention.

The room was silent for a few seconds before a loud round of applause erupted and people began cheering.

When I walked off stage, Leanna said, "Umm, I could look at you and tell you could sing, but DANG, GIRL, you didn't tell me you could shut it down like that! Baby girl, you ate and left zero crumbs!"

I laughed nervously because I genuinely believed I had released something from my past through those lyrics. Even I felt a slight sense of relief, like I had chills running through my body.

I noticed him while I was on stage, before I began singing.

He was brown, with a head full of curly black hair. He had a neatly cut beard and a mustache that was soft and groomed framing his beautiful, full lips.

He turned to talk to someone next to him and flashed a smile, and I almost lost focus. His teeth were so straight and white! Better than Crest and even

Colgate. No, baby, this was that *I spent $100 plus dollars at the dentist getting a professional whitening* set of teeth.

His face alone would be enough to distract me, but his body? Good GOD all day!

Even while sitting, I could tell he was at least 6'2" with a slim, athletic build. Listen, GOD was generous when He created this man.

I was so grateful when I heard them start my music track, because it saved me. GOD may not come when you want Him, but He's always on time. For a moment there, I almost fell victim again. I actually believed I'd dodged a bullet. I didn't have time to get caught up lusting over another man. I'd been single and celibate for the past seven years. Fine or not, even without a wedding ring (yes, I peeped that finger), I was safer sticking to myself.

Leanna and I walked out laughing and talking, making plans to head to another local bar that served food. We were starving.

I made a hard left to walk out the door and walked smack dab into him…

A tall, living, breathing, walking
angel on earth.

Chapter 6

Cameron

"The steadfast love of the Lord never ceases; his mercies never come to an end; they are new every morning; great is your faithfulness."
—Lamentations 3:22-23 (ESV)

With all the money I'd shelled out this year, child support, medical expenses, attorney fees, mediation, proof of payments to Regina's account, I'd spent close to $100,000. And for what? Things still weren't finalized. This was getting downright ridiculous.

Regina knew she was dead wrong. But that girl was stubborn as a mule.

I wasn't trying to take full custody of Carson, I just wanted what was fair. Joint custody and regular visitation. Not the back-and-forth drama, the manipulative games, and the emotional whiplash that had become routine with my psychopathic, narcissistic baby mamma.

"Baby mama." I hated that term.

It felt demeaning, especially given the historical stigma surrounding single mothers. I normally tried to be respectful, especially in relationships, no matter how long or short. But with Regina? That title somehow fit like a glove.

I left the office late that evening, headed to an event at one of our company's venues, a space we used to showcase up-and-coming artists. We'd even had the occasional celebrity pop up, which kept the crowds full and the business booming.

That venue, small as it was, had brought in some of our biggest deals. It sat right in the heart of the city, buzzing with energy.

After a long day, I decided to shower at the office. I threw on a fresh pair of slacks and a crisp, fitted, collared shirt that complimented my lean frame. I drove into work, but when I got to the lot to leave, my heart stopped.

Someone had keyed my car.

Obscenities scratched across the side in angry, jagged letters. I felt heat rise in my chest. I didn't have time to check the security footage, but I already knew, it was probably one of my exes acting childish. Fixing that was going to cost me at least $5,000, maybe more for a full paint job.

Still, I had to shake it off. I was running late and needed to be on time for a meeting we had arranged with a new client. Tonight, was about business.

I mingled a bit, making small talk with current and potential clients. I was in the middle of closing a deal with a well-known street artist whose work on racial injustice had gone viral across the country. Social media had done the legwork, his name was already buzzing.

We were deep in numbers when I heard her.

At first, I just *saw* her.

A rich, dark-skinned woman, chocolate perfection, stepped on stage. She stood there in silence, scanning the crowd. Our eyes met for a brief second, and I thought maybe she was nervous. It seemed that, for a moment, maybe stage fright had crept in.

Then, she opened her mouth.

And my soul *left my body*.

Her voice was silk. Not just soft or smooth, *warm*. A unique blend of vulnerability and strength. She wasn't just singing. She was *releasing*. Every word cut through the noise in the room like it was meant for me.

By the time she opened her eyes again, the crowd was still. No one moved. No one even breathed.

And just like that, it was over.

I hadn't even finished finalizing my deal. But when I saw her walking toward the exit, I knew I had to move quickly. I couldn't let her just walk out of my life before I'd even had the chance to say hello.

I made it to the door just in time, caught her gently by the arms as she nearly bumped into me.

"My bad," she said breathlessly. "I wasn't watching where I was going."

I smiled. "That makes two of us. I should've moved when I saw you coming, but…" I shrugged, eyes locked with hers. "Honestly, I didn't want to."

She blinked at me, caught off guard. Her friend gasped, *loudly*. "Oh. My. God. That man is fine!" she whispered, doing a terrible job at actually whispering.

Tiffeny smiled nervously but didn't pull away.

"I'm Cameron," I said, still holding her arms gently.

"Tiffeny," she replied, sliding her hand into mine.

I made sure my grip was warm, steady, intentional. I wanted her to know I understood how to hold something valuable without breaking it.

"You have a beautiful voice," I told her. "But more than that, you have a powerful story. That song, you didn't just sing it. You *bled* it."

She paused, a flicker of emotion in her eyes. Something I couldn't name. Vulnerability? Hesitation?

"Thank you," she said quietly, almost laughing. "It was personal… maybe a little *too* personal." She shrugged.

"No such thing in art," I replied. "Especially not when it's *that* honest. That was church, therapy, and poetry all in one."

Her friend, sensing a moment, backed away. "Well, I'm gonna get us a table at the spot down the block. Tiff, I'll meet you there?"

We stood, just the two of us, caught in something neither of us knew how to name. A pause. A stare. A silence so loud, it said everything.

Finally, I smiled, softer this time. "If you're hungry, don't let me stop you. But if you ever want to share more of your story… maybe over coffee, a walk, or just some honest conversation with someone who's been through their own version of undoing, I'd love that."

I pulled out my phone and handed it to her, no pressure. Just an invitation.

She took it and slowly typed in her number.

"I'll call you," I said.

She smiled again, her eyes dancing as she turned to leave. "I look forward to hearing from you."

I stood outside the venue long after she disappeared down the block.

This feeling in the pit of my stomach, I didn't recognize.

Usually, when I met a woman and felt attraction, I *knew* that's all it was. Physical. Fleeting. But this?

Tiffeny had me out here feeling like a hopeless romantic. *Butterflies and stuff*, bruh.

What in the actual hell was going on?

I wasn't sure if I should call her… or run for the hills.

Because whatever *this* was?

It felt new, yo.

And maybe a little dangerous.

Chapter 7

Tiffeny

I decided to take Joshua to the park so he could have a playdate with a few of his friends from school. I sat nearby on a bench, watching him laugh and run free while my mind wandered, reflecting on all the lessons that had led me to this very moment… to end up here, in Chicago.

Just sitting and watching him makes me reflect on why I pray often. I pray that God have mercy on my son and not punish him for my sins. That's one of my biggest fears, that the choices I made would follow him like a shadow.

Honestly, since I had him, I've made a conscious effort to live better, to choose differently. I haven't found a new church home yet, but I've visited a few and enjoyed every service so far. I know there's no rush, but I feel I'm getting close to choosing.

I also plan to return to the music ministry soon. I can't sit on my gift too long, not without risking the loss of it entirely.

Since relocating, I've stepped back from social media. People can be cold, ice cream cold. That phrase always makes me laugh bitterly, but it's true. That saying, *"I'm so glad God's not like man"*? Big facts! Because the way folks stay eating me up online…

I'm still receiving hate mail, even though Aliyah, Josiah, and I now have a healthy co-parenting situation. Yes, I say *our* son, because Aliyah is now just as much a part of Joshua's life as his father is. And honestly? I'm grateful. I'm grateful for her acceptance of my son, especially considering the way he came into the world. Aliyah's grace and forgiveness are admirable and beyond commendable.

But the rest of the saints, or shall I say aints… they were still out for blood. Still tearing me down. Still reminding me that my days were numbered, that I'd live with regret and pain for the rest of my life because I almost destroyed a marriage. And for that, I was undeserving of joy, heck, even forgiveness.

And when I sit back and reflect, part of me believes them.

It feels deserved.

I find myself waiting for the karma to come. For it to rip through everything I've built with my son. To destroy the fragile peace we've carved out with the small amount of dignity I had left. I live half-expecting the worst.

When I shared this with Dr. Johnson, she nudged me to remember Jeremiah 29:11(NIV) *"For I know the plans I have for you,"* declares the Lord, *"plans to prosper you and not to harm you, plans to give you hope and a future."*

But do promises like that even apply to people like me?

After all I've done, after all the people I've hurt?

I feel like I *deserve* the financial struggles. The lonely nights in a quiet home once Joshua is tucked in. I even convinced myself I deserved the last terrifying encounter I had.

It was a few nights ago. I'd gone to a lounge alone, just looking for a change of scenery and fully prepared to pay for some overpriced mozzarella sticks. A man approached me. He seemed charming at first. But by the end of the night, he acted like I owed him something for the two drinks he bought and the half-decent conversation he offered.

He started grabbing me in places I never gave him permission to touch, having the audacity to say I was "playing games" and offered to pay for my next weave like that was supposed to be flattering. When I didn't respond the way he wanted, he got downright belligerent, taking cheap shots, saying I was a solid 7 because I had a "cute face, slim waist, thick hips, thick thighs, and a big behind."

I had to literally fight this fool off me. Finally, when this man spit on me and called me a whore and a tease, I lost every bit of my religion and picked up a knife from the table, ready to slice him like a ham on Thanksgiving. Thank God for security! They stepped in before I added aggravated assault to my LinkedIN profile. Thank GOD, because he may not think I'm a ten, but I'm definitely too cute to go to prison.

I felt so violated and humiliated.

I left immediately. I went home, curled up next to my son, and cried myself to sleep. I realized something that night. I wasn't desperate for just any type of attention. Wanting to be seen should *never* come at the cost of your safety. I learned that lesson the hard way. Going out alone wasn't safe for me. Not anymore.

So, the question then is where do people like me fall? Somewhere between karma and grace, I guess. Between *deserving nothing* and still hoping for *something.*

I slapped myself back into reality the other night, after meeting Cameron at the gallery. I mean, seriously… there's no way a man like that could truly be interested in a woman like *me*.

First of all, he was fine, fit, confident, and successful. I wasn't fat, but I was thick. Not the "slim-thick" kind people rave about. Just plain ole thick. The kind that tended to attract the wrong kind of attention—perverts, broken men, or the ones driven solely by lust.

My momma used to teasingly tell me, "Girl, it's all those curves causing confusion with these men. They can't think straight when they see you." I guess that's why I excused it in the past, but no… it's not okay.

For years, I mistook attention for affection, thought being wanted was the same as being worthy. It took too many heartbreaks to learn that not all attention is good attention.

Both married and single, especially the single ones, never chose me. They'd whisper sweet nothings, only to vanish when things got real. In the end, I was always left with a broken heart. Yep, all these curves still couldn't convince a man to stay.

So, I gave up hoping to hear from Cameron.

It had been over a week when, suddenly, my phone rang.

I looked down. An unfamiliar number. Local area code.

I hesitated, then answered.

"Hello," I said softly.

"Hi, may I speak with Tiffeny?" The voice was deep, professional, sexy. It thundered with calm assurance.

"Speaking. May I ask who's calling?"

"Hey, Tiffeny. This is Cameron. I hope I'm not catching you at a bad time."

I laughed nervously. "Oh, no! This is actually perfect timing. I'm just… at the park watching my son pl—"

I stopped mid-sentence.

Had I just let the cat out of the bag? Too soon?

Men hear "*I have a kid*" and start sprinting for the hills. They assume you're messy. A gold digger. That you've got baby daddy drama. All these unfair assumptions.

Funny thing is most of them have their own baggage, but women rarely weaponize it the same way.

I paused. Unsure. Maybe I should let him speak first. But the silence stretched.

So, I broke it. "Sorry. I should've told you sooner, when you first asked for my number at the gallery, that I have a son. Just one. He's six years old and—"

I stopped. I was rambling now. Sounding guilty. Overexplaining.

He chuckled.

"Okay. Maybe one day I'll get to meet him. I have a son, too. His name's Carson. He's nine."

I could hear the smile in his voice. My heart slowed down.

"Really?" I said, surprised, and a little excited. "That's awesome. Maybe one day we can set up a playdate for them."

We both laughed. That nervous, new connection kind of laugh.

We ended up talking for a long time. So long, I'd made it home, given Joshua a bath, and set dinner, all with Cameron still on the phone.

By the end of our conversation, we had a date set.

When we hung up, I stared at my phone for a long minute. My heart fluttered.
He felt… different.
Too good to be true.
There's no way I deserve someone like this, I thought.

The rules of karma say otherwise.

I drafted a text to cancel our date. To retreat into my little safe, quiet corner of the world. I lay in bed, phone in hand, thumb hovering over "send."

I sighed and tried to sleep, still unsure if I'd find the courage to go through with it.

Chapter 8

Cameron

"There are people you meet who, somehow, in a single moment, change everything."

I hadn't realized how long I'd been sitting in the driver's seat until condensation blurred out the city lights on the windshield of my Maserati.

Tiffeny.

Her name hung in the air like incense, familiar, grounding, and laced with something sacred.

We talked for hours, and something in me had shifted. Not because of what she said, though the honesty in her voice was rare, but because of how I felt while she said it.

She mentioned her son, stumbled over it, like she expected me to judge her. I could hear the hesitation, the nervous overexplaining, the bracing for disappointment. I know that tone. I wore it once myself when talking about Carson, trying to cushion the truth so someone else could digest it without gagging.

But with her? I didn't flinch. In fact, I respected her more for it.

I told her about my boy. Carson. Nine years old and the light of my life. And she didn't respond out of politeness. She responded like it *mattered*. Like he *mattered*. That's rare. Really rare.

Most women I'd met, they pretended to be deeply interested in the fatherhood piece, played the nurturing role, but it was a performance. Their focus was my image. My status.

All things surface deep. But not Tiffeny.

She was different. And she didn't even have to try.

I've always been careful with connections. I've learned to guard my softness, wrap it in silence. Regina used my role as a father like a pawn on her board. Other women used me as a steppingstone to boost their own ego or reputation.

So, I learned to guard myself, keep people close enough to smile but far enough they couldn't touch my soul. But with Tiffeny, I wanted to know more.

Who hurt her?
What did she survive?

What does she still whisper to God in the quiet of night?

It's too early to define what this is. I'm not one to chase illusions. But I do believe some souls recognize each other long before the mind can catch up. Maybe that's what this is, two people with matching scars finally finding one another, not in spite of their pain, but because of it.

We've got a date Friday. Just a conversation. No expectations.

I plan to make a real, conscious effort with this one. I can't explain exactly why, but I *know* I should. All the while praying it's not too late. I hope I'm not too late to receive something or someone worth having.

Let's be honest, I've done my share of dirt. I've hurt people. Most of it came from being young and selfish, but some of it came from self-preservation. From shielding myself against a world I knew was full of counterfeit smiles and hollow promises.

My uncle warned me early. Told me to stay ready to swing at all times. To always wear protective gear. To never let anyone get too close. I watched him drink himself into a shell of the man he once was, heartbroken over a woman who ghosted him over twenty years ago.

And now, he's battling pancreatic cancer on top of it all. His pain metastasized, literally.

My parents? They're the rare kind. Solid. Real love. But I never believed that kind of thing was meant for me. I don't do fairy tales. I don't do Disney.

But Tiffeny…

She makes me wonder if maybe, just maybe, there's something sacred left in this world. Something unscripted and honest.
Now, as I sit here, fingers hovering over the screen, I start to type a text. My thumb taps out the words, a potential cancellation dancing between my doubt and my fear.

I toggle between "Send" and "Delete," breath held like a prayer stuck in my chest.

And then, suddenly, I hear my mom's voice in my head. Steady and wise.
"Son, if you're this torn, you need to pray. The Word says, 'Do not be anxious about anything, but in every situation, by prayer and petition, with thanksgiving, present your requests to God.

And the peace of God, which transcends all understanding, will guard your hearts and your minds in Christ Jesus.'" Philippians 4:6-7 (NIV).

I remember.

So, I do what she would tell me to do. I pray.

I give it over to the Lord. Hand it to Him like a novice navigator passing the wheel to the one who knows how to drive in storms. I don't force it. I don't fix it. I don't fear it.

I *release* it.

And then, in that same stillness, I fall asleep.

Chapter 9

Tiffeny

Being a woman who found herself in Christ fresh out of high school, I allowed the church to shape most of my views from that point forward. If I'm being honest, learning who Christ was, and who He still is, has influenced a great portion of my life. But that doesn't mean my past didn't leave its fingerprints on me.

Somehow, the experiences I lived before I really *knew* Him still managed to penetrate deep places in me. And that pain, that history, ended up shaping a lot of the decisions I made, even the ones I thought were rooted in faith.

Dr. Johnson helped me recognize that.

It takes work. Real, gritty, soul-level work, to stop and identify when a thought or an action is being triggered, not by faith, not by wisdom, but by an *automatic trauma response*.

It's not an excuse. That's why I don't share this stuff casually with people. I know I don't owe anyone an explanation for what I'm working through. The only one I owe anything to is Christ. And that's repentance, obedience, and submission. And I've done the hard thing. I've asked for forgiveness from the people close to me whom I've hurt along the way.

I said before that I was being intentional about the life I desire to live. That's still true. But what's also true, and harder to admit, is that deep down, I don't fully believe I deserve for things to be better.

Somewhere along the line, I accepted the idea that romantic relationships would always end in betrayal.

Not because of *me*. I don't cheat. I don't juggle men or play games. That's never been my thing. But I've always allowed myself to be a second choice. A placeholder. A convenience.

That's the worth I used to believe I had. The value I thought I deserved.

Recognizing this toxic belief is part of what's kept me single, and celibate, for years after Joshua was born. I didn't have the strength or desire to go through another situation that would make me question my worth all over again.

I'd entertain the idea of love, sure. But always with a laugh, like a joke I didn't have the courage to take seriously.

And yet… tonight is different.

Tonight, I'm forcing myself to *try*. To step out on faith. To lean into something new, even if it terrifies me.

Joshua is with Leanna until I get back. He's safe. That helps me relax.

So, I get dressed. And while I'm putting my clothes on, all those doubts creep back in, whispering that this is a waste of time, that I'll just end up disappointed, that Cameron will see through me and leave.

What if this gets serious? At some point, I'll have to tell him that my son is a product of an adulterous affair. He'll surely be disgusted with me then.

But somehow, I manage to silence the noise long enough to push myself out the door.

Dr. Johnson's voice echoes in the back of my mind as I walk to the car. She reminds me weekly: grace isn't just for others, it's for *me*, too. That's the part I've always struggled with. Giving grace to others comes naturally. Giving it to *myself*? That's the real challenge.

I arrive at the restaurant early. My palms are damp. My heart is loud.

And then I see him.

Cameron.

He's already seated, checking his phone, completely unaware of the storm he just stirred in me.

Lord have mercy.

I swear I had to *physically* close my mouth with my hand because I was one second away from drooling. This man was *fine-fine.* Like, capital F, fine. The type of fine that makes you want to call your girls and pray in tongues, fine.

And that's when the thoughts came rushing back again. *What if he's too good for me? What if I mess this up before it even starts?*

But right before the spiral begins and I have the opportunity to pivot and turn on my two heels to sprint back out the door, he looks up.

And he smiles.

A smile that tells me I don't have to be perfect. I just have to be *me.*

So, I take a breath.

And I walk toward the table…

Toward possibility.

He stands when he sees me walking over, and Lord, help me, I forgot that this man got the audacity to be tall, too?

"Hey," he says, that smooth, bass-filled voice wrapping around me like a warm blanket that smells like cologne and good credit.

I try to play it cool, really, I do.

"Hi," I reply, flashing what I *hope* is a cute smile and not a "my stomach just did a somersault" grimace.

He pulls out my chair. Sir. Sir. You *not* about to have manners and muscles. It's too much. I *wasn't* emotionally prepared for both. I whine inwardly.

We sit, and for a moment, there's a beat of silence.

A long, quiet beat.

And then I blurt out, "I almost didn't come."

Tiffeny. Ma'am. You could've started with "nice to see you again." Maybe

even "how was your day?" But, no, you
went full confession booth over
appetizers.

Cameron chuckles, tilting his head,
amused but not thrown off.

"Yeah?" he says, leaning back slightly.
"Can I ask why?"

I sigh and think, *because I'm dramatic,
overthink everything, and have an
unhealthy obsession with grilled cheese
sandwiches and childhood trauma.* But
what I manage to say out loud is,
"Because I haven't been on a date in
years, and I didn't trust myself to
pick the right outfit or even be good
company." All that was still a bit
much, but it was better than what I
started to lead with. Thank you, Holy
Ghost, I shout inwardly.

He laughs. A real one. Like I actually
said something funny.

I blink at him. Twice.

He grins. "Glad you still came."

"Me too," I admit. "My therapist said I
need to leave the house more. She
didn't specifically mention dating
former college athletes with perfect
smiles, but I'm sure she'd be proud of
me for trying."

"Oh, so I'm part of your homework?"

"Basically." I nod, deadpan. "You're this week's extra credit."

We both laugh this time, and the tension, at least on my end, starts to melt a little. I realize something I wasn't expecting, I'm comfortable. Not entirely relaxed, but I'm not ready to bolt, either. That's progress.

He asks me how my day was. I give him the edited version, motherhood, work, a little bit of mental unraveling, and one existential crisis while trying to choose an outfit. (Why do I own so many shirts that say "Blessed"?)

He listens. Really listens.

When the waiter comes to take our order, I panic. Why do I suddenly not know how to read a menu? *Macherroni*, I attempt to read silently and not look confused at the same time. Is that a pasta or a skincare product?

"I'll just have whatever he's having," I say, then immediately regret it.

Cameron raises a brow. "So… steak?"

"Oh no, I don't eat red meat."

"Chicken?"

"Only if it's raised in a stress-free environment with lavender essential oils and biblical affirmations playing in the background."

He laughs again, that deep, slow, soul-level kind of laugh that makes my chest ache in the best way. Not the romanticized movie ache, but the *real* kind, like your soul just got seen and gave a little wave back.

He looks at me for a second, like he's trying to figure out if I'm serious or just unreasonably hilarious.

Finally, he shakes his head, smirking. "You're pretty funny, Tiffeny."

I smile and shrug, deciding to lean all the way into the quirk. "Well, you know what Proverbs 17:22 (ESV) says, 'A joyful heart is good medicine, but a crushed spirit dries up the bones.'"

I pause for effect and tap my collarbone with mock seriousness. "And I don't know about you, but I prefer strong bones. Osteoporosis is not on my vision board."

He laughs again, louder this time, and for a split second, I'm a little too proud of myself. But I love that he has a sense of humor.

"I'm starting to see that," he says. "So… joy, scripture, and nutrient-dense food. Got it."

"Exactly," I say, pointing at him like I just finished a TED Talk.

He chuckles. "All right," he says, shaking his head as he looks back at the menu. "I'll help you find something non-traumatic. We'll skip anything that comes with a side of digestive anxiety or moral compromise."

"Thank you. I knew I could count on you," I say dramatically, clutching my chest. "I feel safe already."

"You *should*," he says smoothly, his eyes locking with mine in a way that's suddenly not funny at all, but very, *very* real.

As we continue through the night, it unfolds, full of smiles, laughter, and little moments that feel like seeds being planted.

I don't know where this will lead.

But for the first time in a long time, I feel like it's *okay* not to know.

I'm here.

I showed up.

And if nothing else, that's a win.

(But also, if God wants to let this man text me "good morning, beautiful" tomorrow, I won't fight Him on it.)

Chapter 10

Cameron

It's leg day.

Which normally means pain, sweat, and trying not to cry while pretending I'm just *really focused* on this last set. But today? My brain won't cooperate.

I'm here to train quads and glutes, not daydream like some teenager in a coming of age rom-com. But try telling that to my thoughts, because all they want to do is wander back to *her*.

Tiffeny.

This girl is a problem. I've never been this gone over a woman in my life, on my momma, I haven't.

She's talented. Smart. Spiritual. Hilarious. And hands-down gorgeous. And last night? She had me laughing so hard over dinner, I nearly choked on my steak.

One would think I would have run away scared after she mentioned her seeing a therapist on the first date. Some would consider that to be a definite red flag. But I found it hilarious. She was spilling too much too quickly, like word vomit, obviously because of her nerves. I was totally smitten and intrigued by her.

To me, her honesty about seeing a therapist showed her willingness to be open with me and that she prioritized her mental health. I'm no stranger to therapy. In fact, I'm probably overdue for my next appointment.

She told me early on there were things about her I didn't know, things she'd share when the time was right. That felt fair. We've all got chapters that read a little rough. Some dog-eared with pain. Some redacted in Sharpie. Still, she kept our conversations joyful. Light. Intentional. And somehow, even in all that joy, we got deep.

Tiffeny makes me think about legacy. Commitment. Faith. Love. Things I usually dodge, like those office potlucks at work. I don't know why they keep inviting me, knowing full well I never participate.

It's now seven months in, and we're still going strong. FaceTime, late-night drives after her gigs, prayer over coffee, scripture mixed in with her punchlines.

The wildest part? We haven't even had *that* talk. Nothing sensual, no pressure. It's never been about that. Of course, I notice her. I'm a man. She's gorgeous and sexy, curves and all. But with her, it's not about sexual appetite, it's about alignment.

We've kept it respectful. Disciplined. Friends first.

Now, we're finally planning to introduce our sons. Joshua and Carson. We said we'd wait six to eight months before blending their lives. And here we are. Seven months in, and nothing feels forced.

She's in my prayers, my peace, my playlists. And for once, I'm not looking for the exit. This thing isn't fizzling.

It's catching fire.

Proverbs 31:30 (NIV) "Charm is deceptive, and beauty is fleeting, but a woman who fears the Lord is to be praised." This woman is genuinely funny and naturally beautiful, but not hyper-focused on her looks and always keeping Christ at the forefront of our relationship. It's rare. It's dope.

Chapter 11

Cameron

Saturday afternoon. Sunny, warm, and just chaotic enough to make me question if I packed enough snacks for a United Nations summit. I wanted everything to be perfect.

Joshua and Carson were finally about to meet. We'd picked a kid-friendly indoor play gym—neutral territory. Foam pits, mini basketball hoops, and juice boxes galore.

I pulled into the parking lot and texted her.

Me: "We're here. Carson has his Lebron James jersey on. He's way too excited. He was ready to jump out before I could put the car in park. I had to remind him to pipe down.

Tiffeny: "Mine just told me this is 'the most important day of his life' so I hope your son is emotionally prepared."

She pulled up two minutes later, and I swear, every single muscle in my chest tightened. Not from nerves. From awe.

She was in leggings and an off-the-shoulder sweatshirt, no makeup, her hair in a loose bun. And somehow, she still managed to look like the lead in every daydream I've had for the past seven months.

Carson hopped out of the car first and gave me a very serious nod. "Dad, remember to play it cool. Don't say anything embarrassing. I mean, we don't really know these people. Okay?"

"Got it, sir," I said, saluting.

Tiffeny helped her son out of the backseat. Carson saw him and lit up. "You like DC or Marvel?" Carson asked Joshua.

Joshua blinked. "Both. But Black Panther's the GOAT."

Boom. Instant best friends.

They took off running like they'd known each other since birth. Meanwhile, I looked at Tiffeny and couldn't stop the grin creeping across my face.

"You weren't lying," I said. "He *is* mini-you."

She laughed. "He's actually the reasonable version of me. I'm the dramatic one."

We sat at one of the adult tables near the snack bar, sipping on coffee and watching our boys climb foam towers like they were auditioning for American Ninja Warrior: Kid Edition.

It felt... normal. But also, kind of surreal.

Watching our kids laugh together, team up against the jungle gym, and sneak snacks from each other's bags, it wasn't just cute. It was *sobering in* the best way.

I kept sneaking glances at Tiffeny. The way she watched her son with this protective tenderness. The way she instinctively mirrored both boys' energy and cheered them on while gently correcting them when they got a little too *rough*. She was a natural at motherhood. That was sexy.

She gave a soft smile, one of those that felt like it held about five different meanings.

"I love that," she said, her eyes scanning the play area where the boys were now aggressively negotiating who got the last fruit snack. "It's rare. Joshua doesn't warm up to kids that fast. Usually, he's evaluating them like a tiny therapist."

I chuckled. "Carson usually interviews people like they're applying to be in his Avengers lineup. If you don't pass the vibe check, he's out."

"Well," she said, sipping from her water bottle, "I think they both passed the vibe check. Which means we've got a problem."

"Oh yeah?" I raised an eyebrow.

She leaned in slightly, lowering her voice like we were plotting something illegal. "If this goes south between us… we're gonna have to co-parent their friendship."

I blinked, then laughed harder than I meant to. "So, we'll be those exes at the Chuck E. Cheese birthday party, awkwardly handing out pizza slices while avoiding eye contact."

"Exactly." She grinned. "Except I'm petty. I'd show up overdressed and bring a date just to make it weird."

"Note to self: hire fake girlfriend ahead of time."

We both laughed again and then fell into a more comfortable kind of quiet. The kind that doesn't rush to be filled. Just watching our boys be boys.

Then she said it.

"I've never introduced anyone to Joshua before."

Her voice had softened. Not timid, but honest.

I turned toward her fully. "Really?"

She nodded. "I've had offers. People who wanted to meet him just to get closer to me. But I never let it happen. I always told myself when it felt right, I'd know."

I didn't say anything right away because I knew what she wasn't saying.

And today, it felt right.

"Same," I finally said. "Carson's met women I worked with, friends, you know… safe introductions. But no one I was dating. Not seriously. Not like this."

We looked at each other for a second too long, and everything in me felt like it leaned forward just slightly.

"I'm glad it was today," I said, voice lower than I meant it to be.

"Me too," she whispered back.

Joshua suddenly let out a war cry as Carson launched a foam ball at his chest. The two of them collapsed in a giggling heap.

And just like that, the moment shifted. But it didn't disappear.

It tucked itself quietly into the back pocket of my heart.

Safe. Stored. Waiting for what's next.

For a second, I wasn't a guy with that same guard up. I wasn't thinking about exit strategies or all the reasons I should protect my heart.

I was just... *present*.

Somewhere between spilled Capri Suns and shared gummy bears, something settled in me. Not fear. Not anxiety.

Peace.

Not loud. Not dramatic. Just... still.

Chapter 12

Tiffeny

Over the past ten months, things have been good. So good, they've almost felt… borrowed. Like I've been living in someone else's blessing with no idea when I'll be found out and asked to return it.

Cameron? He's been consistent. Gentle. Intentional. The kind of man who listens, like, really listens… and doesn't make you feel like you have to audition for his affection. But the thing is, he's falling in love with the version of me that I've allowed him to see. Not the whole me. Not the version with blood under her nails and a closet packed with secrets dressed in shame.

Because the truth? I've made choices I'm not proud of. Choices that aren't so easily explained away by "I was young" or "I didn't know better." I *did* know better. And I still said yes when I should've run. I still asked a man who wasn't mine to choose me. I still stayed even after learning he already had someone else. Probably someone who probably prayed for him just like I did.

I wasn't confused. I was selfish.

And that's the part that stings. Not just what I did, but how willingly I did it.

Cameron has told me stories—like the one about his uncle, left shattered by a woman who cheated on him, who never fully recovered. He let that pain rot inside him until it showed up in his body as cancer. Cam shared that story like a sacred warning. Like a ghost tale meant to keep us safe. And here I am, haunted by the possibility that *I'm* that ghost. He also shared on how he dated many women in an effort to keep them at a distance to avoid being hurt.

So how do I tell him? He trusted me with his truth months ago. Why did I wait so long?

How do I say, "I'm not just the girl who sings and prays and quotes scripture. I'm also the woman who once ignored conviction and chose what felt good over what was right."

How do I admit that I've been the exact kind of woman he built his armor to avoid? An adulterer.

This isn't about guilt anymore. It's about integrity. And I can't build a future on a half-truth, no matter how pretty we look in pictures or how strong our kids' friendship is growing.

I want to tell him. I *need* to. But every time I look into those warm, trusting eyes… I freeze.

Because I don't know if he'll see me the same after I strip the mask. I don't know if his love is strong enough, or if I'm brave enough, to risk everything we've built for the sake of transparency.

But if I don't say it soon, the truth will start to decay everything we've created.

And I've lied to myself before.

I refuse to lie to him.

Not anymore.

Chapter 13

Tiffeny

I wish there was a perfect time to say something that could shatter everything.

I practiced it in the mirror. Rehearsed it in the shower. Whispered it in prayer. I even tried to convince myself it could wait—that maybe I was being dramatic. Maybe it didn't need to be said. Maybe my past could stay exactly where it belonged, buried.

But silence is a seed. And I've learned that whatever you plant in silence still grows, usually into something twisted and ugly.

So tonight, I stop hiding.

We're sitting in the car after dinner, the windows slightly fogged from the warm air and our laughter. Cameron had just finished telling a ridiculous story about Carson's soccer game—how he accidentally cheered for the wrong team's goal. I was doubled over, breathless from laughing, when it hit me.

This is the moment.

When everything feels good. Safe.
Comfortable. That's exactly when it
needs to be said.

I turn toward him slowly.

"Cameron…"

My voice comes out too soft, too
careful. I clear my throat. "There's
something I need to tell you."

He stills, instantly sensing the shift.
The smile lingers for a second longer,
then fades. He turns to face me, giving
me his full attention.

Lord, help me.

"I haven't been completely honest with
you. Not because I meant to lie, but
because I was trying to protect what we
were building."

He nods once, slowly. Silent. Waiting.

I take a breath and let it go.

"Before I moved here, before Joshua, I
made some decisions I'm not proud of. I
got involved with someone I knew was in
a serious relationship. A marriage.
They had a son together. And I became…
the other woman. Joshua has an older
brother back in California. His name is
Josiah."

I brace myself. But he says nothing. No twitch in his jaw. No movement at all. Just that unreadable silence.

"I didn't walk away when I found out. I stayed. I even asked him to choose. I wasn't manipulated. I wasn't confused. I was just… broken. Desperate. Selfish."

The air thickens between us. But I keep going.

"I've done a lot of healing since then. A lot of repenting. Counseling. Praying. I've changed. Joshua's father, his wife, and I now have a civil, respectful co-parenting relationship. They've forgiven me. Their marriage and ministry are thriving—stronger than ever."

Suddenly, Cameron's eyes narrow. His voice sharpens.

"Wait a minute, Josiah Williams and his wife Aliyah? They have a son named Josiah?"

"Yes," I answer, confused and stunned. "You know them?"

He scoffs, "They're friends of mine. I visited them years ago. Aliyah was in a broken place, so lost and longing for affection that she… tried to come on to me. Nothing happened. Josiah walked in just in time. But it nearly cost me my friendship with him."

He pauses, then glares at me, realization dawning.

"And now to learn it was all because of *you*?"

His words feel like a slap.

"So that's why you relocated?" he asks, quieter now, but sharper. "Because he didn't choose you? You couldn't bear to watch them live in happiness together, so you took his son and moved to a different state?"

I flinch. Not because he yelled, but because the offense in his words were loud.

"No," I say quickly. "Cameron, I left because I needed to heal. I couldn't grow in the same soil that kept wounding me. I didn't want Joshua growing up seeing me bitter or ashamed or begging for love. I didn't take him out of revenge. I took him to rebuild."

He leans back, rubbing a hand down his face, jaw tight. The energy in the car shifts, like the air itself is holding its breath. I grip my knees and brace for whatever comes next.

"So, you left," he says slowly. "You got to rewrite your story. And you just… never planned to tell me this part? Not even after ten months?"

"I planned to," I whisper. "I wanted to. I was just… scared."

"Of me?"

"Of *us*." I pause, breath trembling. "Of losing something that finally felt real."

He turns away, staring out the fogged window. The silence stretches painfully long.

"You knew my story," he finally says. "You knew about my uncle—how he almost lost everything because of something like this. You let me open up to you. And still—"

"I know," I interrupt, voice cracking. "I'm not here to excuse it. I just… needed you to see who I *am* now, not who I was when I was drowning."

He looks at me then. Not with anger. Something worse.

Disappointment. Uncertainty. And deep underneath, a flicker of hurt.

"I want to believe that," he says quietly. "But I need time. Because right now, I don't know what to do with it. Or with you."

My throat burns.

"I understand," I whisper. "And if you decide you can't move forward with me, I'll still be grateful for what we had. You helped me see myself clearer than I ever have."

He doesn't respond.

And for the first time in ten months, Cameron starts the car in silence.

He drives me home in a hush so heavy, it swallows every word I still want to say.

And yet, somehow, I don't regret telling him.

Because whatever comes next... at least it's built on truth.

Proverbs 10:9(NIV),"Whoever walks in integrity walks securely, but whoever takes crooked paths will be found out."

Chapter 14

Tiffeny

Two weeks had passed and still no word from Cameron. I know I said I wouldn't be upset. I said I would be understanding to him choosing to longer speak to me after learning what I'd withheld from him for so long, but… I lied! This hurt so deeply and so immensely that words can't even express the level of pain and disappointment I was experiencing at that time. I don't believe that it came solely from Cameron's reaction, but it was because I had to say it out loud, in full, exactly what I'd done and how I was moving in the past. It forced me to relive and face the person I'd been who hurt so many people. It took work and counseling to even face my baby who belonged to this married man and not feel my heart ache. I reflect on my past and how at one point, I hit a moment so low and dark, I contemplated ending my life.

I was drinking heavily and regularly, trying to numb the pain and drown my sorrows. I had a note written out and my son's bags packed, ready for him to go live with Josiah and his wife. After all, their marriage and ministry had grown stronger because of the trials they'd endured. They truly allowed God to turn their pain into purpose—no matter how dark it had gotten.

But before I took those pills, Lady Blackwell called me. She asked me to reach out to Dr. Johnson the next day. She said her spirit told her we would connect, and she was certain it could help me start my healing journey.

As for me, I was the culprit, a willing participate who, like her mother, believed that this could still be love and desire and I could still be chosen, no matter who was hurt or how foolish I looked and knew I was being. At the time, all that mattered was that I had something!

And now, years later, these mistakes were still here to haunt me. To punish me and remind me how unworthy, unforgiven, how low I am and clearly not worth redemption. I needed to schedule another session with Dr. Johnson asap. I've been seeing her for four years now. When I was in California, our sessions were virtual. She's one of the reasons I relocated to Chicago. I wanted to see her in-person. After doing additional research about the city, I took a leap of faith and decided to start over.

I was telling Cameron the honest to God truth when I said I wasn't trying to take Josiah's son from him out of revenge. I just had to consider what I needed at the time to be the best mom and in the best condition to raise my son.

I never thought things would come full circle, learning that Cameron knew Josiah and Aliyah. Talk about a twist of fate, and to learn how she came on to him during a low moment from the hurt and pain I'd caused.

I hadn't left the house to go anywhere in days, only to take my son to daycare. I even ordered groceries. I was back in that sunken place, needing to drown in my sorrows of disappointment because it's obviously what I deserved. This darkness and my past mistakes wouldn't leave me alone.

I told myself I wouldn't be upset, that I'd understand if he chose to walk away after learning the truth I'd buried for so long. But I lied.

Because maybe this is what I deserve.

This darkness.

These consequences.

This past that won't let me go.

Chapter 15

Tiffeny

The leather chair across from Dr. Johnson creaked softly as I settled in. It had been a few months since our last session, and the moment I stepped into her office, my chest began to loosen. Not from relief, exactly, but from recognition.

This was the only place I didn't have to pretend.

She gave me that same warm, steady look she always had. Patient. Present. The kind of gaze that could hold a person together without saying a word. "Welcome back, Tiffeny," she said gently. "You've been on my mind. How are you holding up?"

I looked away, tracing the edge of a tissue in my lap.

"I don't even know how to answer that," I whispered. "I thought I was okay… until I wasn't."

Dr. Johnson nodded, letting the silence stretch just long enough to invite honesty.

"I finally told Cameron."

There it was. I just laid it all out on the table.

She didn't flinch. Didn't look shocked. Just kept her eyes on me, gently inviting more.

"I told him everything. About the affair. Joshua's father. The reason I left California. And it, God, it hurt to say it out loud. It was like bleeding from a wound I thought had already healed."

Her voice remained calm, grounded. "And how did he respond?"

I swallowed hard. "He asked me if I took my son out of revenge. If I left just because his father didn't choose me. He looked at me as if I were… disappointing. Untrustworthy."

I took a breath, the words tumbling faster now.

"And out of some sick twist of fate, I find out he knows Josiah and his wife. *Knows* them. In fact, he told me she came on to him during a low moment, when Josiah was living with me. I caused that. I didn't mean to, but it was me. It all comes back to me."

I paused.

Like before, the tears didn't come. Not because they weren't there, but because they somehow didn't feel deserved. Crying would've felt like I was asking for sympathy. And this? This was my mess.

So, I just sat there. Silent. Exhausted. Life had been whooping me, and I was too tired to fight back.

"Did that feel familiar?" Dr. Johnson asked.

The question broke something loose.

"Yes," I breathed. "It felt like my mother. Like being thirteen again, watching her scream at the mirror, asking why none of the men stayed. Like I was becoming her."

Dr. Johnson leaned in slightly. "How so?"
I paused, unsure of how to answer her. How do you explain a lifetime of quiet unraveling in a sentence or two?

Sensing my hesitation, Dr. Johnson gave me space and then gently redirected me. "Talk to me about your dad. You shared that he left your mom for another man when you were…" she glanced down at her notes, "nine years old. How did that make you feel?"

I let out a humorless chuckle. "How did it feel to know that my dad left my mom to start a romantic relationship with Uncle Eric?"

She stayed quiet and calm, knowing the question was rhetorical and that I wasn't done.

"My whole life, I've wondered—were we really that bad? My mom and me? Were we so unlovable that he could choose a man over his own family? Did he ever love us? Why have sex with my mom? Why bring a child into the world just to walk away?"

I felt my voice unintentionally rising, sharp, and bitter.

"And then, to make it worse, to have me call his 'close friend' Uncle Eric? That's not just confusing, it's sadistic. It's sick!"

I hadn't noticed the tears until they were already pouring.

Hot. Relentless. Uninvited.

The memory alone still felt suffocating.

"He never even tried to come back home. Not even for me."

I swallowed hard. "I got a letter on my twelfth birthday. From my dad, apologizing. He said he believed I'd be better off without him. That he didn't deserve my love. He didn't deserve me."

I scoffed, bitter and broken all at once.

"He was a coward. Selfish. And…" I paused, my voice cracking, "and I still wanted him to be there. I still needed him."

I wiped my face, angry at the tears, angry that after all these years, they still came so easily. It had been a long time ago, something I thought I'd buried deep enough to forget.

When I turned eighteen, tired of witnessing my mom's toxic relationship cycles, I left town on the first thing smoking. I hustled hard, working side jobs, and earned an associate's degree in social and behavioral science. I wanted to build a better life for me and my son.

I cut contact with my mom. I couldn't continue watching her destroy herself for men who obviously cared nothing for her.

A few months before I earned my degree, I got the call.

She was gone.

One of her latest beaus, who was high and out of his mind, robbed her, shot her six times, and stole her car.

I couldn't bring myself to attend the funeral.

That night, I vowed that by any means necessary, I'd never be like her. I'd create something real. A life with love, marriage, and a family. But only with a man who was undoubtedly deserving.

"So, my mother… It was pretty obvious that she never got over it. Man after man, she chased them like they were the cure. Getting their attention was never the problem. But keeping them? Choosing a man of quality was almost impossible for her. That was the pattern. And I think, no, I *know,* it chipped away at her. At her self-worth. Maybe mine, too."

I paused, letting the words hang in the room. Then I whispered, almost to myself, "Maybe that's why I feel like I'm becoming her. I've never been able to keep a long-term relationship. I try, but it never lasts. I think I'm turning into my mother."

Dr. Johnson tilted her head. "Do you really believe that? That you're becoming your mother?"

"I try not to," I admitted. "But when Cameron looked at me like that… when he didn't call or text after I told him… it felt like confirmation. Like the shame was right. Like I really don't deserve anything whole or lasting."

We sat in the weight of it. In the ache.

"And yet," she said gently, "you told him anyway."

I blinked, caught off guard.

"You didn't have to," she continued. "You could've stayed quiet. Kept hiding. But you didn't. That tells me the woman sitting here now isn't the same woman who made those choices years ago."

I looked down at my lap, her words slowly sinking into the cracks I thought I'd sealed with regret.

"I wanted to be honest," I said quietly. "I wanted to build something real."

"And you did," she said. "Even if it broke something in the process. Truth doesn't always bring peace right away.

Sometimes, it has to clear the wreckage first."

I nodded, brushing away the tears with the tissue I'd been clutching since I walked in. "I just didn't expect the silence to hurt this much."

"Silence can feel like punishment," she said. "But it can also be someone else's processing. You gave Cameron something heavy, Tiffeny. You can't carry his response *and* your healing at the same time."

That part hit like a whisper from God Himself.

"I've been spiraling," I admitted. "Not eating. Not sleeping. I started writing a letter… not to anyone else. For Joshua. Just in case. Just in case I couldn't keep pushing through."

Dr. Johnson's expression softened, her eyes warm but steady.

"Thank you for saying that out loud," she said. "You survived that moment, Tiffeny. And you chose to be here. To sit in truth. That matters."

I nodded, slower this time. My breathing, finally, began to steady. "I just need to know that redemption is still possible."

She smiled, kind but firm. "Redemption isn't a reward for perfect people. It's a promise rooted in love—*despite* imperfection."

And for the first time in weeks, something inside me lifted.

Not completely. Not permanently.

But enough to get me through the day.

And maybe, for now, that was enough.

Psalm 103:12(KJV) "As far as the east is from the west, so far has He removed our transgressions from us."

Chapter 16

Cameron

Three weeks.

That's how long it's been since I last saw her face, since I heard her voice crack open the quiet with truth so sharp, it cut through everything I thought we were building.

And still, I couldn't stop thinking about her.

I told myself the silence was necessary. That I needed time to sort through what she told me, to separate my emotions from my logic. But the truth was… I was scared.

Scared of how much I still wanted her despite what I now knew. Scared that if I spoke to her too soon, I'd either say something I couldn't take back, or worse, forgive her too easily and pretend like none of it mattered.

But it did matter.

She knew my story. She knew about my uncle—how infidelity nearly destroyed him. How watching him halfway fight for his life made me swear I'd never let myself, or anyone I loved, walk blindly into that kind of destruction.

And she sat in front of me that night and admitted… she was *that* woman. The other woman. The one who caused someone else the kind of pain I'd spent most of my life resenting.

And yet… what shook me more than her confession was the pain in her eyes. The way she spoke, like she already hated herself enough for both of us. Like she'd been living in that shame longer than I could comprehend.

I didn't know what to do with that.

And in the same breath that I was judging her… I had to check myself.

Because the truth is I've made my own share of mistakes.

I've hurt women. Pushed good people away because of the things I saw growing up. I became emotionally unavailable, unreliable—sometimes even reckless. So how dare I sit in the seat of judgment, acting like her past is more unforgivable than mine?

Still… I was open with her. She waited this long to be open with me.

And now I can't help but wonder what else she might be hiding, what other truths she's tucked away just to keep herself protected.

I don't want to be cynical. I don't want to doubt someone I've grown to love. But the silence between us has fed every insecurity I've tried to bury.

And the worst part? I can't shake the feeling that this is exactly what I deserve.

Maybe this is the future I built from all the selfish choices I made in my past. Who am I kidding?

I'm no prince charming.

This is karma.

First, Regina. Then my cars keep getting keyed—like the universe is keeping score. And now… this.

I'm afraid to ask what's next. Afraid to hope for something better. Maybe I should just sit in this sorrow. Drown in the darkness. Because maybe that's what men like me get in the end.

Maybe this is all I was ever meant to have.

I sat at work, waiting to hear from Regina about picking up Carson. Hours passed. No text. No call. I tried ringing her phone. No answer. Called again. And again. Four times. Nothing.

I sent messages. Still nothing.

I even called Regina's mom. Straight to voicemail. Who was I kidding with that call? That woman despises me. Ever since Regina cried to her about being pregnant, I've been enemy number one. I'm sure I've been blocked.

Panic crept in slowly, then all at once.

I reached out to a friend of mine on the police force. Told him Regina was over 24 hours late bringing Carson to me. I explained that I'd given her grace, held back from panicking, believing she'd call or show up at any moment. But now? Now, it felt different.

I couldn't take it anymore. Regina needed to answer for why she hadn't brought my son to me. It was *my* time. And she knew that.

Anger boiled over. Every part of me radiated with it.

My friend promised to make some calls and get back to me.

Those two hours were the longest of my life.

When he finally called, his voice was calm but heavy. "Cameron… she left town."

I went quiet.

"She left?" I repeated, trying to process.

"Yeah. And since she's Carson's legal parent and there's no formal custody agreement on file… legally, she can do this."

He didn't have to say anything else.

She could get away with this.

Because we never finished the paperwork. Never made it official.

I saw red.

I started throwing whatever was in reach, papers, my phone, a lamp. I punched the wall, then another. And still, nothing brought relief. Nothing made me feel better.

I dropped to my knees.

I broke. No more pride. No more pretending.

Just a man, on the floor, desperate for grace. Desperate not to be punished through the one thing he loved more than anything else.

Romans 12:19(NLT) "*Dear friends, never take revenge. Leave that to the righteous anger of God. For the Scriptures say, "I will take revenge; I will pay them back," says the LORD.*"

Chapter 17

Cameron

Over a month had passed. No calls. No texts. Not a single word from Regina. Until—

Ding. A text alert.

I looked down. Regina.

The message was short. Cold. "We need to talk."

Typical Regina. Always the one to dictate the terms. Always needing control.

The *audacity* of her, to disappear with my son, vanish without a trace, and then pop back up like *she* had the right to demand a conversation.

My fingers trembled as I typed back, "Regina, where in the hell is my son?!"

A moment later, another message. "We need to talk. Meet me at the Corner Café at 4 pm."

I stared at the screen. I wanted to unload on her. Let her feel the fire she lit in my chest. But I knew myself. Knew that anything more would turn into

a string of curse words and rage I
couldn't reel back in.

So, I stopped. Breathed. Put the phone
down.

Just see your son, I told myself.
That's all I could focus on. The rest
would have to wait.

4:00 PM

I pulled up to the café, palms sweating
against the steering wheel. I scanned
through the glass windows and saw her
sitting inside, calm as ever. She was
sipping coffee like she didn't just
turn my life upside down. Like she
hadn't ghosted me for thirty days while
holding my son like a pawn in some
twisted game.

No guilt. No urgency. No shame. Just
Regina. Unbothered.

I got out of the car, jaw tight, every
muscle in my body screaming for
release. I walked in, straight to her
table.

She looked up and smiled faintly, like
this was a casual catch-up. Like we
were old friends.

I leaned in, fists clenched, trying
like hell to control my tone.

"Where is my son?"

She didn't flinch. Just lifted her cup to her lips and took a slow sip.

"Relax, Cameron. He's fine. He's with my cousin."

"*Your cousin?*" I echoed, stunned. "You disappeared over a month ago, ignored every call and message, and now you're sitting here like everything's normal, telling me he's with some cousin I've never met?"

She tilted her head, still calm. Too calm.

"I needed space. Time to think. And I didn't feel like explaining myself to you while I was sorting things out."

My voice rose, despite myself.

"You took my son. That's not needing space, that's *kidnapping*, Regina."

She narrowed her eyes, and her voice dropped to that sharp, patronizing tone she loved to use. "Don't be dramatic. I'm his mother. And legally, there's no custody agreement, remember? So technically, I didn't do anything wrong."

I stared at her in disbelief, my fists clenched so tight, my knuckles turned white under the café lights.

"This is *my* son too. You don't get to make that call on your own."

She leaned back, crossing her legs slowly.

"Which is exactly why we need to talk. I've been thinking, and I'm willing to make things work… under the right conditions."

I laughed. Bitter. Tired.

"Conditions? After what you pulled, you want to come to me with *conditions*?"

She nodded like it was business.

"Yes. Because whether you like it or not, you still want to see him. And I'm willing to give you that… if we come to an agreement."

My heart was pounding, rage thick in my chest, but somewhere beneath all of it, was something else, fear. The fear of what she could take from me if I didn't play this right. The fear of losing my son all over again.

So, I sat. Swallowed my pride. And listened.

Because sometimes, strength isn't in the shouting. It's in silence and standing still.

Regina crossed her arms and leaned forward slightly, lowering her voice just enough to seem sincere with manipulative sincerity, her specialty.

"I know about Tiffeny," she said.

That name hit the table like a dropped glass.

My body tensed. "What?"

She smirked just slightly. "One of my friends saw y'all out together a while back. Said you looked real cozy. So, I put two and two together."

I didn't respond. Didn't owe her confirmation.

She kept going. "You see, Cameron… part of why I left was to think about what's best for Carson. He needs *stability*. He needs *structure*. And he needs his parents under one roof."

I stared at her, disbelief rising in my throat.

"You're not serious."

She blinked slowly. "I'm completely serious. We were something once. And we made a child together. Maybe that was God's way of pushing us back where we belong."

"Regina, we were never 'something'. I apologized for leading you on, but I never loved you in that way. If you're honest with yourself, you didn't love me in that way, either. You couldn't have. I never gave you enough to fall in love with. It's the money, security, and status you want. Be real right now. You don't care about me! You weaponized our son against me, and now you want to play house? Stop with the games, Regina. It's time to grow up!"

She raised an eyebrow. "I'm willing to forgive the past." She continued as if she didn't hear a word I just said. "I'm offering us a second chance—for Carson's sake. That means no more Tiffeny. No more confusion. Just us, as a family."

I felt my jaw lock. My fingers curled into fists again under the table.

"And if I say no?" I asked.

She looked me dead in the eyes.

"Then I can't guarantee when, or if, we'll move back to Chicago. I don't want him growing up in limbo. He needs a full-time home, and if you can't give him that with me…" She shrugged. "I'll have to make a decision that's in his best interest."

No shame. No apology. Just emotional blackmail, sugar-coated as maternal concern.

I shook my head slowly, the ache in my chest spreading like wildfire.

"You're not thinking about him. You're thinking about control."

She scoffed, "Believe what you want. But those are my terms. Take them or leave them."

For a split second, I saw it all laid out, ending with me giving in, playing the part, hating myself every day, slowly fading into the version of a man I swore I'd never be. A hollowed-out shell, trying to fake a family for the sake of appearances. Living a lie so I could see my son.

But then I thought of *Tiffeny*. Her honesty and courage, even in her brokenness.

She didn't use her pain to manipulate me. She faced it. Owned it. Spoke truth even when it cost her everything.

2 Timothy 1:7(NKJV) "For God has not given us a spirit of fear, but of power, and of love, and of a sound mind."

And here I sat, across from a woman who hadn't faced anything. Someone who just rerouted wreckage to get what she wanted.

I looked at Regina and stood to my feet slowly.

"You don't get to decide my son's life like this. You want to co-parent? Fine. But if this is your version of a family, I'll fight for him through the courts. You're not going to hold my son hostage because you're threatened by the fact that I've moved on."

She laughed under her breath. "You think a judge is going to side with *you?* The man with no agreement in place and a history of flings and failed commitments?"

"I don't need a perfect past to be a present father." My voice was calm now. Dangerously calm. "And I'm done negotiating with terrorists."

She narrowed her eyes. I turned and walked out, heart pounding—but not from fear this time.

This was war.

And I'd fight with everything in me.
Not just for custody, but for *peace*.

Chapter 18

Cameron

I'd be lying if I said I didn't miss her. Day and night, I found myself thinking about her and worrying about how she was really doing.

Tiffeny wasn't the kind of woman who craved pity. If anything, she fought too hard to pretend she was fine. But I knew better now. I remembered how she once told me she went through a season of alcoholism.

She wasn't trying to escape the world. She was trying to escape *herself.* All the shame. All the guilt. All the weight she carried for the decisions she couldn't undo.

And I… I added to that weight.

She trusted me with her truth, and I held it like evidence against her. Instead of listening with compassion, I listened with suspicion. Instead of embracing her vulnerability, I used it to question her character.

I had no right to do that.

And now, here I was, neck-deep in a custody battle, emotionally spent, spiritually stretched, and still aching for her. Not just her presence. Her laugh. Her stubborn strength. But also… her forgiveness.

She left the ball in my court. Didn't chase. Didn't beg. Just *waited*. And I left her there. Hanging in silence while I spiraled through my own storm.

But even in the chaos, I couldn't shake her voice. The way she said, "I just need to know that redemption is still possible."

It is. And I want to be someone who reflects that, not just for her, but for myself.

I pulled out my phone, thumb hovering over her name in my favorites. My heart thudded like I was about to make the biggest gamble of my life.

And maybe I was.

James 4:14(NIV) "Why, you do not even know what will happen tomorrow. What is your life? You are a mist that appears for a little while and then vanishes."

So, I hit call.

It rang once… twice…

Chapter 19

Tiffeny

I almost didn't answer.

The phone rang, with his name lighting up the screen, and my first instinct was to let it go to voicemail. Not out of anger, but protection. From the hope that had already burned me once. From the feeling that maybe, just maybe, he'd finally seen me and not just my past.

But something in me… a whisper, said, "*Try.*"

So, I picked up.

"Hello?"

For a moment, all I could hear was his breathing on the other end. That familiar silence that used to comfort me suddenly felt heavy. Like both of us were balancing everything we didn't say on the thin wire between us.

"Hey," he said finally, his voice low and… softer than I expected.

I didn't know how to respond, so I didn't. I let him speak.

"I'm sorry."

Those two words cracked something open in me I didn't even know was still frozen.

"I've been… dealing with a lot. With Regina. With Carson. It's been hell, honestly." He exhaled, like the weight was crushing him even as he confessed. "But that doesn't excuse how I left things between us."

Still, I said nothing. Because hearing it wasn't the same as believing it. But I kept listening.

"You told me the truth, and I judged you for it. You gave me something raw and real, and I didn't handle it with care. That's on me."

I closed my eyes. The tears didn't fall, but they sat there, ready, if I let them.

"I've been thinking about you. About everything you said. About how strong you had to be just to face it, let alone say it out loud. And how I didn't match that strength."

Finally, I spoke. "Why now?"

His pause was honest.

"Because I was scared," he said. "And because I'm tired of punishing someone who already did the hard work of healing. I've been praying, asking God if I should try again… if *we* should try."

"I don't know if I trust you," I said honestly, voice barely above a whisper.

"I don't know if I trust me, either," he admitted. "But I'd rather try and fail than keep pretending I'm okay without you."

Silence again.

Not the heavy kind this time. The kind that asked… *Could we?*

I didn't say yes. I didn't say no.

But I didn't hang up, either.

And maybe, for now, that was enough.

We sat in silence, two people who knew brokenness, but who also believed in redemption.

Sometimes healing didn't look like a grand moment.

Sometimes, it just looked like willingness to try.

Romans 8:25 (NIV) *"But if we hope for what we do not see, we eagerly wait for it with patience."*

Chapter 20

Tiffeny

As I sit and ponder the conversation I had with Cameron, I'm reminded of words I hear from Dr. Johnson.

"I'm going to say something that may sting," she began, folding her hands gently on the table. "But it's said in love."

I look up to face her, holding my breath and bracing myself for the delivery.

"I recognize the level of unforgiveness you're carrying. And I don't just mean for others," she said, her voice calm but clear. There is still unforgiveness or pain you are carrying from the pain your mother may have caused and, most importantly, the unforgiveness you carry for yourself."

She looked at me.

"I've watched you fight shame like it's your shadow. You give grace to others, explain their pain, understand their why. But when it comes to you? You bury yourself under regret and call it accountability."

"But that's not how God works," Dr. Johnson said, voice firm. "Yes, the universe responds to what we sow. We can't pretend like choices don't have consequences. But the enemy has a way of twisting consequence into condemnation. And when that happens, you stop growing. You stop healing. You start speaking curses over your own life."

She paused, letting it settle.

"Self-pity is seductive. It makes you feel righteous in your suffering. But if you stay there too long, it becomes self-destruction. You mistake silence for justice. And you call it karma, when really… it's just fear dressed up in spiritual language."

My throat tightened.

Dr. Johnson continued, in a gentle voice. "You're allowed to grieve what happened. You're allowed to be disappointed in yourself, in each other. But what you're *not* allowed to do is give up on your healing just because you don't think you deserve it. Grace doesn't skip over the one who caused the pain. It reaches *for* you, even when you think it shouldn't."

I press, even now, a hand to my chest, as if trying to hold the words in place.

"And remember," she added softly, "God's grace is not conditional. It's not earned. It's not karma. It's love. And it's sufficient, even for this."

For a while, sitting there, neither of us said anything.

Dr. Johnson shook her head slowly. "Hurt doesn't redeem. Only healing does."

As I allowed myself to consider these words and how Cameron showed kindness, grace, love, and a peace offering, I allowed myself the chance to believe I deserved something new and something possibly real.

Galatians 5:22-23 (NIV) "But the fruit of the Spirit is love, joy, peace, forbearance, kindness, goodness, faithfulness, 23, gentleness and self-control. Against such things there is no law."

And maybe, just maybe, something new could grow through the broken places.

Chapter 21

Cameron

Tiffeny and I had been going strong for the past few months. Almost too good to be true. I'd even regained custody of my son, Carson. My attorney came through like a pit bull, shredding Regina's narrative in court. The judge saw through her. We provided photos and statements documenting how little time Regina spent with our son and how she left Carson with her mom and cousin more than she cared for him herself, how she withheld my visitation out of spite. In the end, the court granted me sole custody, with Regina receiving visitation rights. In the end, she wasn't upset at all. She'd already begun dating some NBA player and had already moved in with him. So, she got the life she was looking for after all… or so time will tell.

For the first time in a long time, things were finally turning around.

Today, Tiffeny met me at my office so we could ride to the park together. A simple afternoon. Peaceful. I met her downstairs, and we laughed about how she was always five minutes early just to prove a point.

We were walking toward my car when I heard it, tires screeching in the distance. Fast. Reckless.

Tiffeny and I both paused, trying to locate the sound.

Then came the gunshots.

Pop. Pop. Pop.

Time froze.

I stood still a second too long, stunned, until instinct kicked in. I lunged toward Tiffeny, tackling her behind my car, the freshly painted Maserati. She hit the ground with a thud, and I landed over her, shielding her body as the chaos tore through the street.

Screams erupted. More shots rang out before the car sped around the corner and disappeared.

Sirens wailed in the distance, growing louder.

I let out a shaky breath. "You okay?" I asked, not even sure if I could hear myself.

But she didn't answer.

That's when I felt it.

Warmth.

Wet.

I looked down.

Blood.

My palms were slick with it. And Tiffeny wasn't moving.

No. No. No.

"Tiffeny?" I whispered, already panicking. "Tiffeny, talk to me!"

She was still. Eyes shut. Lips parted.

"Tiffeny!" I shouted, shaking her, harder than I probably should have. "Baby, stay with me! Please!"

People crowded around. Phones up. Voices blurring together. But all I could see was her. All I could feel was her blood.

I pressed my fingers to her neck, desperate to feel a pulse.

Come on, God. Please.

A paramedic finally knelt beside us. "We've got a weak pulse!" he shouted. "We need to move, now!"

They loaded her into the ambulance, and I climbed in beside her without thinking. I grabbed her hand. Cold. Too cold.

"Keep talking to her," the EMT said. "Let her hear you."

So, I did.

"Tiffeny," I murmured, "you said this place felt like home. Don't leave it, baby, don't leave me."

I stared at her face, beautiful, fragile, and growing pale.

"I'm sorry," I whispered. "For everything. For the way I reacted. For not calling. For not fighting for you sooner. I need you. Do you hear me? And I love you. I don't know when it happened, but I love you."

I blinked through tears. "You don't get to leave me like this. Not now. Not when I finally got it right. Not when we just found our rhythm."

The sirens kept blaring. The city blurred by.

And I kept holding her hand like it was the only thing tethering me to reality.

If this was karma, it had come for the wrong one.

Because I knew now, God doesn't trade in vengeance the way we do.

He doesn't break us to punish us. He breaks us open to rebuild us.

And as long as Tiffeny had breath in her body, I would be there.

Not as her punishment.

But as her promise.

Chapter 22

Cameron

By the time I got back to the hospital, Tiffeny was awake and fully conscious.

The second she saw me walk through the door, she cried out, panic rising in her voice, "Cameron! Where is Joshua?! Where's my baby?"

Instinct took over. I rushed to her side and held her tightly as she sobbed in my arms.

"Joshua's fine," I whispered, gently rocking her. "He's with Leanna. Safe. We haven't told him anything yet. I wanted to wait for your permission."

Her body trembled against mine, and I tightened my grip, burying my face in her hair as I breathed in the relief of her being alive. "The doctors said you're going to be okay," I added. "The bullet was a through and through. By God's grace, it missed every major artery."

I pulled back just enough to look into her eyes. "You're going to be just fine."

My voice cracked on the last word.

"Tiffeny…" I choked, my throat thick with grief and fear and everything I'd been holding back. "I'm so sorry, baby."

She looked at me with that same softness that undid me every time. It carried gentleness, love, and empathy, all swimming in her eyes. "It's okay, baby," she said, reaching up to gently wipe away my tears. "It's my fault. It's not your fault—"

"No." I cut her off sharply, pain ripping through every syllable. "No, it is my fault."

Her head tilted slightly to the side, her gaze urging me to go on, though she said nothing.

I swallowed hard. "The woman who shot you…" My voice dropped to a near whisper. "It was someone I was involved with in college. A girl I hurt. Badly. Her name is Kierra."

"The police caught up with her a few blocks away from the shooting," I continued.

Tiffeny blinked, silent, listening.

"I was in my selfish era," I explained. "Arrogant. Careless. She loved me. I took her virginity, and I used her like she didn't matter. I broke her heart and never looked back. She ended up needing therapy. Had a breakdown on campus. After that, I just wanted to look away and pretend none of it truly happened. I never checked on her. I never looked for her, to apologize and attempt to make things right. I just… moved on."

I shook my head, ashamed. "A few weeks ago, she reached out to me online. Sent a long message… said she'd seen me out with you. I ignored it. Thought if I didn't engage, it would all just go away, like before."

I looked at Tiffeny, eyes burning. "I didn't realize she was still carrying that kind of pain. I didn't think she'd—God—I never imagined she'd do something like this."

Tiffeny reached for my hand, her touch as steady as ever, even while lying in a hospital bed recovering from a gunshot wound.

"I brought this danger into your life," I said, my voice hoarse. "Because of the man I used to be."

Her grip tightened. "And who you *used to be* is not who you are now," she whispered.

I looked down, ashamed. "But it doesn't change what happened."

"No," she said gently, "it doesn't. But, Cameron… you're not God. You don't get to carry the weight of someone else's choices on your back forever. She didn't shoot me because of *who you are*. She did it because of *what she never healed from*."

I shook my head, stunned by her grace.

"Baby," she said, pulling me close until our foreheads touched, "if we keep letting our past write our future, we'll always be stuck in fear. You can't live like that. I won't let you."

Her words reached a place in me that no sermon, no friend, no self-help book ever had.

This woman was shot because of my sins, yet she was holding me like *I* was the one who needed saving.

And maybe, in a way, I was.

Psalm 103:2-5(NLT), "Let all that I am praise the Lord; may I never forget the good things he does for me. He forgives all my sins and heals all my diseases. He redeems me from death and crowns me with love and tender mercies. He fills my life with good things. My youth is renewed like the eagle's!"

Epilogue

Tiffeny

Some stories don't end with a fairytale kiss or some dramatic plot twist. Some stories end with quiet healing. With scars that no longer sting. With two people who've learned to love in truth and not in perfection.

It's been seven months since the day I nearly died in Cameron's arms. The day pain from his past collided with pain from mine.

But today… Today, I am his wife.

We exchanged vows in a small chapel filled with close friends, family, and the Holy Spirit. There were no fireworks. No choreographed first dance. But there were tears. So many tears. Because everyone in that room knew the journey we'd both been on to get to this moment.

Looking back, we used to live in fear. Not just fear of people, or of consequences, but fear of karma. Fear that our past mistakes would always find a way to destroy our joy.

But here's what we've learned: Karma is not the final judge. God is.

Yes, we've faced consequences. Yes, we've reaped what we sowed in many ways. But we also reaped mercy. We reaped healing. We reaped a love that was refined through fire.

For so long, we carried guilt like it was a badge of honor. We believed we were supposed to suffer, to live in emotional scarcity because of the damage we'd done or survived. We forgave everyone but ourselves, then wondered why our hearts kept bleeding.

But through counseling, prayer, and honest surrender, we finally saw the truth. Self-pity isn't humility, it's a trap. Shame doesn't protect you, it poisons you. And calling our pain "karma" was just our way of punishing ourselves when we were too scared to believe in grace.

God doesn't work on a point system. He's not waiting to strike us down with lightning every time we mess up. He *restores*. He *rebuilds*. He brings beauty out of ashes. And when we finally accepted that… our healing began.

Cameron and I still face judgment. There are people who whisper about the past. People who think we don't deserve the peace we now walk in. But that's okay.

We weren't called to be perfect. We were called to persevere. And the storms we've weathered together have only made our foundation stronger.

There will be more storms; of that, I have no doubt. But now we walk into them with open hands, with open hearts, and with a God who's already gone ahead of us.

Our love isn't built on fairytales. It's built on forgiveness. On truth. On grace.

And that... That's more than enough.

Romans 5:2-6(NIV), "Through whom we have gained access by faith into this grace in which we now stand. And we boast in the hope of the glory of God. Not only so, but we also glory in our sufferings, because we know that suffering produces perseverance; perseverance, character; and character, hope. And hope does not put us to shame, because God's love has been poured out into our hearts through the Holy Spirit, who has been given to us. You see, at just the right time, when we were still powerless, Christ died for the ungodly."

About the Author

Brandy Lynette is a storyteller with a heart for healing and a gift for writing stories that sit in your soul long after the final page. Her work explores the raw edges of faith, trauma, redemption, and the journey to becoming whole.

She is the author of *The Test and the Turnaround,* and her sophomore release, *Cases of Karma,* is a deeply reflective novel about shame, generational wounds, and the grace that still pursues us when we think we're too far gone. Brandy writes for those who've survived quietly, for those who wonder if healing is still possible, and for anyone brave enough to begin again.

A devoted mother of three sons, Brandy lives her life rooted in purpose, prayer, and the belief that stories, when told truthfully, can set people free.

Another Book By This Author